HOLE D
IN THE SKY

Godless
Invisible
Mr. Was
No Limit (formerly titled *Stone Cold*)
Sweetblood

Published by Simon & Schuster

HOLE
IN THE SKY

PETE HAUTMAN

SIMON PULSE
NEW YORK   LONDON   TORONTO   SYDNEY

For Kurt, Cindy, Alley, and Jerod

SIMON PULSE

An imprint of Simon & Schuster Children's Publishing Division
1230 Avenue of the Americas, New York, NY 10020

Copyright © 2001 by Pete Hautman

All rights reserved, including the right of reproduction in whole or in part in any form.

SIMON PULSE and colophon are registered trademarks of Simon & Schuster, Inc.

Also available in a Simon & Schuster Books for Young Readers hardcover edition.

Designed by Anahid Hamparian

The text of this book was set in Perpetua.

Manufactured in the United States of America

First Simon Pulse edition November 2005

10 9 8 7 6 5 4 3 2 1

The Library of Congress has cataloged the hardcover edition as follows:

Hautman, Pete, 1952–

Hole in the sky / Pete Hautman.

p. cm.

Summary: In a future world ravaged by a mutant virus, sixteen-year-old Ceej and three other teenagers seek to save the Grand Canyon from being flooded, while trying to avoid capture by a renegade band of Survivors.

ISBN-13: 978-0689-83118-8 (hc.)   ISBN-10: 0-689-83118-8 (hc.)

[1. Grand Canyon (Ariz.)—Fiction. 2. Science fiction.] I. Title.

PZ7.H2887 Ho 2001

[Fic]—dc21

00-058324

ISBN-13: 978-0-689-84428-7 (pbk.)   ISBN-10: 0-689-84428-X (pbk.)

ACKNOWLEDGMENTS

I want to thank my hiking companions and technical advisors, Greg Corman, Kurt Dongoske, and Joe Hautman, for their company, and for sharing their eyes and ears and expertise. Thank you to Jim Justham, Jason Raucci, and Morgan Phillips of Canyon Dreams Backcountry Guides and Outfitters for getting us in and out of the biggest hole on the planet. Thank you to Mike Mitchell, who gave me a great deal of accurate information about infectious diseases, much of which I distorted to serve my own dark purposes, and thank you to Bob Marley for sharing his experiences hiking the Little Colorado River gorge. And thank you, Mary Logue, for reading this book four or five times, and for everything.

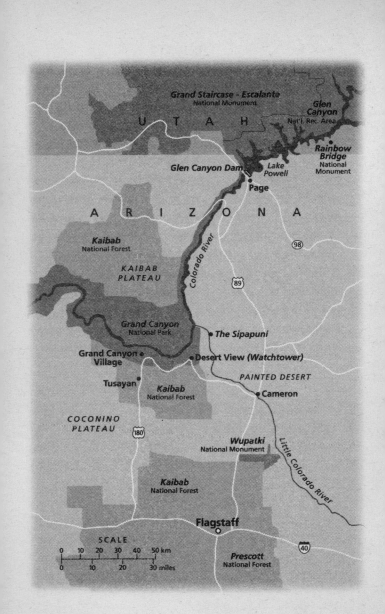

CONTENTS

PROLOGUE

On November 2, 2028, during KLM Flight 3851 from Paris to New York City, an eighteen-year-old Ethiopian soccer player named Worku Roba complained of a mild headache, which he attributed to pressure changes in the Boeing 747 cabin. The flight attendant brought him an aspirin and a bottle of mango juice.

Roba and his teammates were scheduled to play an indoor exhibition game the next day at the Meadowlands. This was their first visit to the United States.

Shortly before the plane landed at JFK, Roba began coughing. He reassured his teammates that it was nothing, just a bit of peanut caught in his throat.

Between the time he disembarked and the time he checked into his room at the Omni Central Park Hotel, it is estimated that Roba came into contact with thirty-four other people.

At three o'clock the next morning, Roba's roommate made a frantic call to the front desk, shouting, "My friend is coughing blood!"

At 3:47 A.M., Roba was checked into the emergency room at Bellevue Hospital. Seventeen hours later, his ravaged lungs ceased to function, and Worku Roba was pronounced dead.

Four days after Roba's death, the entire Ethiopian soccer

team and everyone else on Flight 3851 came down with a similar flulike illness, as did several airport employees, the taxi driver who had transported Roba to the Omni Central, seven of the hotel staff, six nurses, three doctors, and nine patients from Bellevue, and a panhandler who had asked Roba for a quarter.

All of them died.

The mutant virus was cataloged as influenza D/Ethiopia/28 (H43N32) by the Centers for Disease Control and Prevention in Atlanta, Georgia. Within the CDC, the new disease was dubbed Grunseth's Flu, after the first researcher to die of the virus. On the streets of New York City, where, within two weeks, more than seven hundred thousand people were infected, it was more commonly called the Ethiopian Flu.

In Ethiopia, where the disease had been killing people for several weeks, it became known as the Somali Flu, because it was believed to have been brought into their country by Somali refugees. In Somalia it was called the Chinese Flu, because the first televised warnings to the populace were delivered by the Chinese doctor who ran the government hospital in Muqdisho. In China, the sickness was rumored to have been brought on by a clandestine biological weapons assault, and was named the American Flu.

Every country had its own name for the pandemic, but all agreed on one thing—the disease was more virulent and deadly than any the world had known. Long before they realized they were ill, victims of the disease became highly contagious, spreading the virus with every handshake, every kiss, every breath. The first symptom was usually a dull, throbbing headache, followed by a nagging cough. Within a day or two the virus would settle deep in the lungs, producing a form of hemorrhagic pneumonia. Once the victim began to cough up blood, death inevitably followed.

That first winter, more than five billion people died.

Another nine hundred million people died the following winter and, late in 2031, a third wave of Grunseth's Flu took another seventy million people. By that time, Earth's human population had spread out thin enough to prevent any major outbreaks. Still, the Flu continued to be a threat, especially in larger communities. When it did strike, rapid and ruthless quarantining procedures were employed, reducing the contagion rate. Dogs, pigs, and ducks, all believed to carry the virus, were shot on sight. Because contact with strangers carried considerable risk, many communities barricaded themselves, posting guards who were quick to challenge anyone who approached their positions.

No single community, however, could be 100 percent self-sufficient. Trade between groups continued, and elaborate methods for "safe trading" were developed. Bartering was carried out in large, open areas where the traders were required to remain at least fifty feet away from one another. Trade goods were left in the open for a full twelve hours, the length of time the virus was believed to survive outside of a human host. A simple trade—say, a half ton of wheat flour for a working John Deere tractor—could take a full day, and might involve several armed and suspicious men.

A more common and efficient form of "safe trading" was through the use of Survivors.

On average, for every two thousand people who contract Grunseth's Flu, only one will survive. These individuals, known as "Survivors," do not develop hemorrhagic pneumonia but, instead, suffer a form of post-infectious encephalitis, which often results in some degree of blindness, deafness, or loss of the sense of smell.

Survivors who suffer only the loss of their senses are the lucky ones.

Many Survivors are left with impaired mental functions—slowness of thought, severe depression, and delusional thinking are common. Approximately 8 percent of these Survivors become violent and/or suicidal.

Nearly all Survivors were between the ages of eleven and eighteen when they contracted the Flu. Without exception, Survivors lose their body hair, including their eyebrows. It has been suggested that those who survive the Flu do so because they carry a rare but widespread mutation, a theory which remains unproven but popular with today's scientific community.

As of this writing there are an estimated 1.3 million Survivors worldwide. One hundred thousand of them live in North America. Fewer than half of those are able to care for themselves.

Survivors continue to hold a special status in post-Flu North America. Because they have developed immunity, they cannot spread the disease. Survivors can travel from place to place without endangering others, and are often used in trade situations. Survivors are valuable, but they are also envied and sometimes resented by those still vulnerable to the ravages of the Flu. As a result, some higher-functioning Survivors have banded together into their own communities, notably in the southwestern United States, where one small band of renegade Survivors known as the Kinka are said to have actually attacked neighboring communities.

By 2036 the decline in Earth's population had slowed to a net loss of approximately 3 percent per year. As of this writing, the estimated world population stands at thirty-eight million, an average of one person per square mile of livable land, most of them residing in scattered communities of one hundred people or fewer. The Flu continues to take lives, with new outbreaks occurring every few weeks, as the search for a vaccine enters its second decade.

—from *A Recent History of the Human Race* by P. D. Boggs © 2038

Part One:

CEEJ

TIM

I STAND AT THE EDGE OF THE WORLD.

Between me and the north rim lies twenty miles of space and a billion years of rock. I have lived here for more than half my life, but I still get this feeling in my gut. The canyon fills me with emptiness. Wind whips up the canyon walls, inflating my lungs, cool and clean, scented with juniper and pine. Below, I see layers of limestone, shale, granite. Red, green, gray, and a thousand shades of brown.

The wind shifts and pushes me toward the abyss, the canyon beckoning, drawing me toward its gaping maw. The longer I stare into this vast chasm, the more unreal it becomes, like a postcard or a dream. The north rim seems closer now. I could reach out a hand and touch it. I could step off into space and find beneath my feet an invisible walkway, a bridge of thought. I feel its pull.

"Ceej!"

I blink, startled. The panorama before me wavers, and I take a step back.

"Get your butt over here with that brush!"

I look down at the brush in my hand, then back at Uncle and the mules. He is working on Frosty, brushing her down, checking for ticks. Cecil, our other mule, is watching me, waiting for his turn. Cecil and Frosty are brother and sister. They were born sixteen years ago, the same as me. They are the last surviving Grand Canyon mules, part of a herd that once carried tens of thousands of tourists up and down the Bright Angel Trail, from the luxury of the El Tovar Hotel to the crude stone cabins of Phantom Ranch.

Now they have only me, and Uncle, and my sister, Harryette.

I begin to groom Cecil, beginning with the backs of his huge, hairy ears. They make me think of Tim.

I met Tim when we were just little kids, and the first thing I noticed was how far his ears stuck out. Like a mule looking at you. Later, Uncle told me, the rest of him would catch up.

"Take my nose," Uncle said. "When I was a boy I used to worry my nose was too big. But then I grew up and everything sort of fell into place."

Uncle had one of the hugest noses I ever saw, but I didn't say anything. When you only have an uncle like Uncle and a big sister like Harryette, you learn to keep your trap shut.

Tim's ears were not only big, they worked good, too. He could hear anything. One time I found him watching a bunch of ants dragging a green caterpillar up the side of a stump. "Listen," he said.

Tim was my best and only friend.

When I first met Tim we were both eight years old. Harryette and I had been living at the south rim of the Grand Canyon for a few months. One day I was helping Uncle mend the corral fence and I heard the distant putter of an engine. Uncle, whose ears weren't so good, heard it a second after me.

"Defense," Uncle said. We ran back to El Tovar, the hotel where we lived. Uncle grabbed the 30-30 carbine and took up his station on the porch, just outside the double doors leading into the front lobby. He knelt behind one of the stone arch windows and trained the rifle on the bend in the driveway. I had never seen Uncle shoot anybody, but I knew he'd do it in a second if the wrong person came into view. Harryette, who had been cleaning a basket of pine nuts, saw what was happening. She grabbed a shotgun off the rack and ran to the loading dock at the back of the hotel. I'd never seen Harryette shoot anybody either, but she was at least as mean as Uncle, and a lot jumpier. Me, I'd have rather come in the front way.

I got an extra rifle from the cabinet and waited with it behind Uncle, ready to hand it to him if he ran out of bullets. This was our Defense plan. Shelter, water, food, defense—those were the four things Uncle drilled into us again and again.

Just before the vehicle came into sight, the driver honked his horn three times, and I saw Uncle's shoulders drop down, the tension gone out of him. The three honks meant it was Hap Gordon, the trader. But Uncle kept the gun sticking out the window until he could see the dusty, dinged-up body of Hap Gordon's Jeep poke its nose around the bend. Hap's Jeep was almost fifty years old, same as Uncle's Land Rover. The old twentieth-century engines were easier to fix.

We all ran out to greet him. Hap showed up once a month or so with medical supplies and other assorted trade items. You never knew what he would have. One time he had a case full of cigars. Uncle bought a box and stunk up the hotel for weeks. Another time Hap sold us a pony, which didn't last as long as the cigars. The wolves got him.

Hap climbed out of the Jeep. He had a beard this time, but otherwise looked the same as always: small and wiry with squinty blue eyes, wearing jeans, a checkered flannel shirt, and a beat-up old straw hat over long gray and black hair tied in a ponytail.

Emory, a Survivor who traveled with Hap, got out of the passenger side. Emory was the opposite of Hap: tall, thick, wide-eyed, and, like all Survivors, totally bald—no eyebrows, no nose hairs, nothing. His face was slack and sorrowful, which was normal for him. Both his skin and his eyes were the color of wet earth. According to Hap, Emory could talk when he had something to say, but I'd never heard him speak a word. Mostly he just stood around looking sad and dopey. He had survived the Flu without losing any of his senses, but it had taken something else out of him.

But it wasn't Hap or Emory that interested me. It was the smaller creature climbing from the back of the Jeep.

This time, Hap had brought along a kid.

Hap said to the kid, "Tim, this is the boy I was telling you about. His name is C. J. They call him Ceej." Hap smiled at me. "Ceej, this is my son, Tim."

Next thing I knew, Hap and Uncle and Emory were walking into the house, leaving me with this weird-looking, green eyed, big-eared kid. Tim was the first kid I'd seen since Harryette and I had come to the Grand Canyon. I didn't know what to do, so I just stood there and scowled at him. He scowled right back.

What I did next was really stupid and I don't know why I did it. Who knows why kids do the things they do? I picked up a rock and threw it at him.

I missed.

Tim said, "Now it's my turn." He bent over and scooped up a rock about the size of a raven's egg.

I ran away as fast as I could. I got to my secret place up in the top floor of the old Hopi House gift shop and just hid there with all the spooky kachina dolls and spider webs and moth-eaten blankets until, an hour or so later, I heard the Jeep start up and roll away down the driveway. I figured I'd seen the last of him, but of course I figured wrong. I climbed down and went into the house to see what Hap had traded us this time, and when I saw what was there, well, you could've knocked me down with a breath.

Uncle and Harryette were sitting at the kitchen table cutting up a chocolate bar. Now I love chocolate as much as anybody, but I didn't love what else was sitting there at that table. It was too weird. This was even worse than those cigars.

It looked to me like Hap had traded us his kid.

That was how I met Tim. A few days later we got to be best friends. Of course, it turned out that Hap hadn't really traded him to us. He'd just left him to stay with us for a while. When Hap and Emory came back a week later and Tim climbed into his Jeep and they drove off, I was sorry to see him go.

After that, every time Hap would make his run from Phoenix to Flagstaff to Page, he'd swing by Grand Canyon Village and leave Tim with us for a few days. I always looked forward to his visits. Tim was a real character. He always had ideas for things to do, and we hardly ever got caught. Although I'd have to say that I got in more trouble when Tim was around than when he wasn't.

I remember one summer we decided it would be fun to roll some rocks off the rim of the canyon. We pushed a few big ones over and watched them crash down the rock face, smashing through scrub oak and juniper trees, crushing smaller rocks, and finally coming to rest or disappearing from sight. Tim had his eye on this one rock. Actually, it was part of the canyon rim, a chunk of Kaibab limestone the size of Hap's Jeep. Between the rock and the edge of the canyon was a crack about ten inches wide. Tim figured it was about to break away. He thought when it went, it might crash all the way down to the river.

"I don't think so," I said. We were standing at the edge looking down into the canyon.

"You don't want to do it?"

"I just don't think it could roll all the way to the river." We could see a tiny section of the turquoise ribbon far below—the Colorado River. "That'd be more than ten miles. I don't think it could go that far. There's all kinds of places for it to get stuck."

"Yeah, but it's so big!" Tim said. "It would crash through *anything!*" He was in love with the idea of sending that rock over the edge.

Tim just didn't comprehend the size of the canyon. Even with it spread out in front of him he didn't understand how huge it was. That rock was no more than a mouse turd to the Grand Canyon.

But when Tim got an idea, he wouldn't let go.

He found an old hydraulic jack in the transportation building and talked me into helping him haul it to the rim in a wheelbarrow. We wedged the jack down in that crack and started pumping. At first the rock wouldn't budge. It must've weighed about fifty tons.

But Tim got a long metal pipe and stuck it on the jack handle for leverage and we both threw our weight against it. With a ragged groan, the rock moved about an inch.

"Yes!" Tim shouted, his face red with effort and excitement. We wedged some smaller rocks down into the crack to hold it, then repositioned the jack and went at it again.

We worked on that rock for three days. Every time we got stuck or busted a jack, Tim would find another one in an abandoned truck or car. And every time we were about to give up, that rock would move another quarter inch. The crack between the rock and the rim kept getting wider until it was big enough to crawl into. We had four jacks crammed down in there.

On the third day the rock shifted, only in the wrong direction. All four of the jacks got scrunched, and that rock just sat there laughing at us.

"That's it," I said, flinging the jack handle off the edge. "This is stupid." We heard the jack handle clang against the rocks a hundred feet below.

Tim stood there scowling.

"We can get more jacks in Tusayan," he said. Tusayan was the town six miles to the south. No one lived there anymore, but it was full of old cars and trucks.

"I don't want to go to Tusayan." The place was creepy. The houses were full of skeletons. Last time I was there I saw a coyote with a bone in its mouth. I was pretty sure it was some little kid's arm bone.

"Then I'll go myself."

"You're stupid. This thing isn't gonna move." I jumped across the crack and stood on the rock. I stomped my feet on it; it felt solid as a fifty ton boulder. "This rock's gonna be here for another million years," I said.

That was when the earthquake hit. Except it wasn't an earthquake at all, it was the rock moving, and I was standing on it. I saw Tim's eyes go wide, and the sky seemed to tilt, and the air filled with thunder. I must've jumped, because the next thing I knew I was lying on my belly on the rim and the rock was sliding down the face of the cliff. Tim's mouth was open and he was screaming or shouting but all I could hear was the grinding, booming, eardrum-shattering sound of the canyon giving up a chunk of its rim. Tim looked out over the edge to watch; I got on all fours and scrambled in the opposite direction. The roar continued for what seemed like forever. Sound waves echoed up from the canyon as the enormous boulder smashed smaller rocks and splintered trees.

As the sound faded I could hear Tim yelling, "Go! Go! Go!"

And then it was over, except for faint echoes returning from distant buttes.

Tim leaned so far out over the brink that I thought he would go next. "Cool!" he said.

· · ·

Ten minutes later I was still shaking.

The rock never made it to the river. It had skidded down the face of the rim, tore a ragged path through a forest of stunted pinyon pine, oak, and juniper, crashed through a limestone ledge a few hundred feet below, cut a gouge through the layer of pale sandstone, and come to rest on a wide shelf about six hundred feet below us. On its way down, the rock had dislodged several of its smaller brothers, which continued to tumble and slide. The roar of the avalanche went on for half a minute, and the echoes for even longer.

I thought Tim would be disappointed that our big rock hadn't reached the river, but instead he was inspired. All the way back to El Tovar he talked really fast. He knew where there was another rock, an even bigger one. Me, I could hardly talk. I'd almost gotten killed. Besides, the Grand Canyon was big enough. I didn't want to make it any bigger.

"I bet we could find some dynamite someplace," Tim said.

We were almost to the village when we ran into Uncle and Harryette. Uncle looked worried.

"Did you hear that?" Uncle asked.

"Yeah," Tim said. "We were right by it. A huge avalanche!"

"Thank God! I thought for a second that the dam had gone."

He was talking about the Glen Canyon Dam, one

hundred miles upriver. Uncle was obsessed with the dam. If it ever failed, he liked to say, the river would rip the guts out of the canyon.

Uncle liked to worry about the canyon. He was a Grand Canyon National Park Ranger, the only one left alive. Even though nobody paid him or even knew he was alive—as far as we knew, the government didn't exist anymore—he still wore his uniform. He figured the Canyon was his responsibility. You couldn't so much as stomp on a tarantula without him blowing his stack.

"Show me," he said.

Uh-oh, I thought. Harryette, silent as always, had a little smile on her face, like she knew what was coming. She thought it was funny whenever I got in trouble with Uncle.

She signed, *What did you guys do?*

Tim, who had picked up some sign language from Harryette, signed back: *We made the canyon bigger.*

Tim was always trying to impress my sister. He once told me he thought she was "a real looker." Something he'd heard in a movie once. Personally, I couldn't see it.

Since there was no way around it, Tim and I walked with Uncle and Harryette back to where we'd sent the rock on its journey. It took Uncle about two seconds to figure out that hunk of limestone hadn't jumped off the rim on its own. He saw our footprints and the broken jacks on the rocks below. He turned to me and drew back his hand as if he was going to hit me.

I hoped he would. I hoped he'd hit me hard. If he smacked me a good one, that might be the end of it. But something in his eyes glittered and he lowered his hand.

"Charles Jacob Kane," he said, shaking his head sadly, "you have disappointed me."

I knew then that Tim and I were in for the most severe punishment imaginable.

We were going to have to listen to one of Uncle's lectures.

Uncle was a man of few words—except when you got him started about the Canyon. For nine years, ever since Harryette and I had come to live with him, he'd been teaching us about the Grand Canyon. We knew the names of the rocks, the plants, the animals. We knew the life cycle of the desert tortoise, the safest way to descend a talus slope, and when to harvest the fruit of the banana yucca. It took three million years for the Colorado River to carve out the Canyon, and that was about how long Uncle would have kept talking about it if he didn't have to eat and sleep.

This lecture started off with a detailed description of the damage we had done. Uncle went over the geological history of the rock we had moved, and of the older rocks below it. He talked about the trees and other plants that had been uprooted, shredded, and crushed. He told us how many hundreds of years it took a juniper tree to grow, and how many animals relied on the acorns from the little oaks, and how many decades it would be before the lichens we had scraped from the canyon wall could renew themselves.

We were sitting in the lobby of El Tovar, surrounded by the stuffed heads of dead animals: deer, javelina, elk, pronghorn, and an enormous moose we called Bullwinkle. Uncle paced back and forth in front of the dead fireplace, talking. I'd heard it all before, but I knew that if I didn't look like I was listening he would give me a whack on the head. A couple of times during his lecture he got so worked up he whacked me anyway, but not very hard, just a tap. Harryette, sitting off to the side, was reading a book and smiling. Every now and then she would catch my eye and make a silent joke with her hands. *Look at the little glob of foam on Uncle's lip. You think he's got rabies?* She was trying to make me laugh, so I'd get hit again. I bit my cheek, holding it back.

Uncle kept talking for more than an hour. He told us about how the Canyon had once been clean and pure, and then the Spaniards had come and gazed upon it with greedy eyes, and then John Wesley Powell had run the river from top to bottom, and then the miners had riddled the canyon walls with holes, and then the tourists had come with their gum wrappers and cigarette butts and beer cans, and then the dam had been built and the Canyon was all but destroyed.

It was thoughtless people like us—he pointed at me and Tim—who had almost wrecked the most beautiful place on earth.

I felt a yawn coming on, so I bit harder on my cheek. I must've made a face because Uncle stepped over and rapped the top of my head with his knuckle. What really fried me was that the whole thing had been Tim's idea, and he never got hit once. At least not by Uncle. I looked at Harryette. She was watching me with her I-told-you-so smirk. I looked up at Bullwinkle the moose. He seemed to be smirking, too.

All that happened, I guess, about three years ago. Tim got me in plenty of trouble after that—like the time we got into Uncle's wine supply—but the avalanche was the biggest and noisiest stunt we ever pulled.

Tim was trouble, but we always had fun.

HARRYETTE

TIM AND HAP HAD BEEN on a trading circuit for more than three months when Uncle got a call on his CB radio that they were back on the plateau and would be arriving in two days. I was eager to see Tim again. Except for Uncle and Harryette, I hadn't seen another human being since March. But I was also a little nervous. Tim always showed up with stories of adventures and amazing sights, and I always felt like boring old Ceej, just sitting around Grand Canyon Village cutting wood and feeding the mules and losing games of gin rummy to my sister.

So I started thinking about ways I could impress him, and I came up with the idea of fresh fish. Except my idea wasn't really about fish, it was about heading down the Bright Angel Trail. All the way to the river. Alone. Fishing was just the excuse, and the fish were how I'd prove that I'd done it.

The more I thought about it, the more I liked my idea. Tim and I had talked about riding down to the river, but we'd never done it. Uncle thought it would be too dangerous for a couple of irresponsible kids. The Bright Angel had once been a wide, well-maintained trail, but since the Flu it had fallen into disrepair. Several areas were washed out and hard to follow. I wasn't worried, though. I'd explored the upper parts of the trail hundreds of times, and I'd ridden down to the river twice before with Uncle, so I knew what I was getting into. It was a long mule ride—a good three hours just to get down, and about five hours to climb back up, but I figured if I left early enough I'd have time to catch some trout and be back on the rim for dinner. Uncle might not even miss me. Or maybe he would, and I'd catch hell, but that didn't seem important at the time. I imagined myself talking to Tim over a dinner of fried rainbow trout: "Yeah, I just figured I'd ride down the Bright Angel and snag a few." Like it was nothing.

The predawn air was chilly, only a few degrees above freezing. It would be a lot warmer down in the canyon. I saddled Cecil. He had a mind of his own, but he was the younger and stronger of our two mules. I loaded the saddlebags with a pair of four-liter plastic water bags, a fishing rod, and a bag of pine nut-butter sandwiches. Cecil was too sleepy to make much of a fuss, but just to make sure he stayed quiet, I fed him a handful of dried apple rings. You wouldn't think a mule would care what it ate, but Cecil had his favorites, and dried apples were at the top of his list. I led him out of the corral and walked him quietly past Kolb Studio to the trailhead.

Kolb Studio was a two-story wooden building pasted to the edge of the canyon like a glob of food stuck to the rim of a water glass. A few months earlier, on her nineteenth birthday, Harryette had moved out of her rooms in the El Tovar and into Kolb Studio. She said she needed a place of her own. Uncle had made no objection. He knew better. Harryette pretty much always got what she wanted.

The Bright Angel Trail passed directly below the studio. I walked Cecil the first few hundred yards. I didn't want to wake up my sister. The last thing I wanted was for her to tell Uncle what I was doing. I waited until we were out of earshot before climbing onto the saddle. Cecil let out a sputter of protest and stamped his feet a few times. I leaned over his thick neck and fed him another apple ring, then urged him on down the trail.

The sky began to lighten in the east. The canyon spread out before me, filling my heart. I had lived on the rim half my life, and I'd been down in the canyon dozens of times, but the feeling of riding down into that enormous slash in the earth remained undiminished. Three hundred miles long and one mile deep, the Grand Canyon could make a grizzly bear feel tiny and insignificant. To enter the canyon was an act of faith. I had to trust the canyon, and myself, and Cecil the mule. If all three of us cooperated, I'd return to the rim alive. With fish.

The first hours of our descent were uneventful.

The trail had washed out in a few places, but Cecil was surefooted, and with a little coaxing we made it past the bad spots. Soon the sun lit the top of Shiva Temple, the largest butte to the north, and then brightened the pointed, bone-colored summit of Shiva's lesser neighbor, Isis Temple. As we approached Indian Garden, sunlight spread across the Tonto Platform, two miles away and five hundred feet below me. I could see the Tonto Trail, a ribbon of pale brown twisting and rippling across the soft gray-green of the platform. This was farther than I had ever come on my own. I stopped and unzipped my jacket; it was getting warmer. I felt exposed and vulnerable, but also energized and determined to complete my journey. I listened to the sound of wind on rock, and a faint hiss that may have come all the way from the river. I even heard the distant echo of Cecil's hooves on rock—or was I hearing something else?

Turning in my saddle, I saw a mounted figure coming down the trail behind me. I knew who it was right away because the sun had risen just high enough to glance off the top of her bald head. Harryette. My stupid sister had saddled up Frosty, our other mule, and followed me.

She stopped about two hundred yards back and made a circle with her arms over her head, asking me if I was okay. Instead of returning the signal to let her know all was well, I turned my back and continued down the trail. Harryette had been telling me what to do my whole life, and I was sick of it.

This was supposed to be a solo journey. I didn't ask for company.

Harryette followed me all the way to the river. I took the trail upstream, past the suspension bridge that crosses the river to Phantom Ranch, an old, abandoned tourist camp across the river. I'd been there once with Uncle, and I hadn't liked it. According to Uncle, Phantom Ranch was named after a Havasupai ghost that had come up from the underworld. The Havasupai Indians were all dead now, so maybe there were a lot of their ghosts hanging out in the canyon, but we hadn't seen any. It was spooky enough with all the collapsing stone buildings full of black widow spiders and rattlesnakes.

That same trip, Uncle and I had caught some trout just below the small rapids a few hundred yards upstream. I followed the trail to the rapids. They looked different. In fact, the whole river looked different. Instead of the rushing, noisy torrent I remembered, the river had become a quiet, burbling brook. The jumble of boulders that formed the rapids were sticking up out of the water, their sides slick with algae. I could have rock-hopped all the way across the river. Strange.

I walked Cecil upstream to a sand spit to let him drink, then tied him to a small tamarisk tree.

Harryette watched me, shaking her head. She made a motion with her hands, telling me I hadn't tied him good enough. I ignored her. I didn't need my sister telling me how to tie a knot. Ever since our parents died, she'd been bossing me around. I was sick of it. This one time I'd wanted to do something by myself and here she was, telling me how to tie up a mule. I unloaded the fishing rod and went hunting for bait.

The best bait for big trout, according to Uncle, was a live scorpion. I set about turning over rocks. There are a lot of scorpions in the canyon, and it only took a few minutes for me to find a big fat one. I held it down with my boot and used my pocket knife to lop off its stinger. A couple years ago I stepped on a scorpion with bare feet and I couldn't walk for a week, so I didn't feel too sorry for this one.

I stuck it on a hook, then walked downstream a few yards and threw the line out into a pool. Harryette tied Frosty to a mesquite tree, then came up and stood beside me. She was about two inches taller than me, but I was catching up fast.

The water is low, she signed. *They must have closed the dam off up at Page.*

"You're ugly and bald," I said.

Harryette just stood and frowned, watching my line where it entered the water. If she'd understood what I'd said she'd have thrown me right in the river. But there wasn't much danger of that. Spoken words meant nothing to Harryette. She couldn't understand me, and she couldn't speak a word. Harryette was a Survivor.

Uncle is going to kill you, Harryette signed, standing in front of me so I could see her hands.

I ignored her, but she knew I'd read her signing. Harryette had taught herself sign language from books, just after she'd woken up from her coma and found out that she couldn't talk. Whatever part of the brain that turned sounds into words had been fried. People who got the Flu mostly died. But not always, and the ones who survived were always kind of strange. Harryette could still read and write, but she couldn't speak or understand spoken words.

She'd taught me and Uncle to sign. I was better at it than Uncle.

The Flu had changed her in other ways, too. Back when we lived in Phoenix, Harryette had been a cheerful seventh grader who talked constantly. She was always busy with her school work or her singing lessons or designing clothes that she would sew herself. She'd wanted to be an actress and a singer. She had been my best friend, even though she was almost four years older than me. Then the Flu came to town. One day everything was okay—and three weeks later everybody we knew was dead.

Our parents saw what was happening before most people. They kept us quarantined. When things got really bad in Phoenix—dead people everywhere—we headed north in the Land Cruiser. The plan was for us to stay with my uncle in Tusayan, a small town just south of the Grand Canyon. Dad said the farther we got from the big cities, the safer we'd be. I don't remember a lot of my life before we came to live with Uncle, but I'll never forget that drive. The freeways were clogged with crashed and abandoned cars. A few miles outside Phoenix some men tried to run us off the road, but we got away from them in the Land Cruiser. After that, we stayed on the little, twisty roads. Every small town we came to was a ghost town.

We were driving through a place called Williams when Harryette started to clear her throat and cough. We stopped and Mom took me to an empty house and gave me a bunch of food and water and told me not to come out until she came back for me. I didn't understand what was happening, but I stayed in that house waiting for Mom and Dad to come back. I think I was in there a week. Finally, I went out to look for them.

I walked around that town for hours. Except for a small herd of pronghorns grazing on somebody's front lawn, I saw nothing alive. I returned to the empty house.

The next day, I went out again. I was walking down the main street when I saw this bald kid sitting in front of a house eating a box of cookies. I went over and asked him if he had seen my mom and dad. The kid just looked at me with this weird expression and all of a sudden I recognized my sister, only with no hair. I said her name, but she wouldn't answer me. She just kept staring at me with blank eyes. She hadn't said a word but, somehow, I had known in that moment that our parents were dead.

After that, everything changed. The old Harryette had disappeared. All the new Harryette wanted to do was read books. When Uncle drove to Flagstaff to scavenge gasoline and supplies, he would bring back stacks of books from the bookstores. Harryette read them all. She would read anything. The new Harryette, the one watching me fish, didn't sing or talk anymore. She was a Survivor, but the Flu had killed something inside her.

I felt a tug on my line. I jerked back on the rod to set the hook, then started reeling in. I could tell it wasn't a big fish, and when I pulled it up onto shore I'd caught a sucker about six inches long. Waste of a good scorpion. I threw the fish back and went looking for another scorpion.

Harryette had found a patch of shade beneath a mesquite tree. She scraped a depression in the sand in front of a granite boulder and settled into it.

Angrily, I signed at her to go away. She signed, *You are going to be on kitchen duty for a month.*

The most irritating thing about my sister was that she was almost always right.

The sun was almost straight overhead and the temperature had climbed into the eighties by the time I caught my first trout. Harryette clapped and smiled.

I couldn't help but grin back at her. After that I caught one almost every time I threw my line in the water. It was harder finding the scorpions than catching the fish, but I soon had six brightly colored rainbow trout, more than enough for dinner.

Harryette asked me how I was going to keep the fish fresh during the long climb back to the rim. I'd been wondering that myself, but I figured if I wrapped them in fresh leaves and grass and put them in my T-shirt and soaked it with cold river water, they'd be fine. We'd be back on the rim in four or five hours. Cecil could make good time when he had a meal waiting for him. I looked back at the tamarisk where I'd left him.

Cecil was gone.

Cecil's tracks led downstream, clear arcs impressed in the soft sand. I was furious with Cecil for taking off, and even madder at myself for not tying him better. Harryette and I followed the tracks for an hour before losing them on a stretch of bare rock.

You are in trouble, Harryette signed. Her mule wouldn't be able to carry both of us, and it would take me a good eight hours to climb to the rim on foot.

"We're gonna find him," I said.

Harryette cocked her head. I signed to her to head back upstream, in case we'd missed him. I would continue to follow the river west.

Not safe, she signed. *Stay together.*

I shook my head and started walking again. I'd stay

in the canyon the rest of my life before I'd tell Uncle I'd lost a mule. Harryette hesitated, then shrugged and walked back the way we had come.

After another hour of searching, I again found the marks of Cecil's shod hooves. That stupid mule could really move. At that point the walls of the gorge came right up to the river, and I had to climb a slope of broken rocks. I couldn't see Cecil's tracks on the rock, but it was the only way he could have gone. I finally found a sheep trail with more of Cecil's tracks. For some reason he had stopped and trampled a small area, breaking rocks and scuffing the earth as if something had startled him. Just as I was wondering what had happened, I heard a buzzing noise that tingled my skin from the back of my neck all the way to my toes. Without moving my legs, I searched the ground around my feet, my heart pounding.

There, less than a yard away, a coiled rattler, dusky pink with rust-colored markings, its tail a vibrating blur. Holding back the urge to run, I slowly moved one leg in the opposite direction, planted my foot, then followed it with the other one. The snake continued to buzz. I took another step—six feet away now, I began to relax. Rattlers can't strike beyond their body length, and this one was only about three feet long, but I kept my eye on it until I was a good twenty feet away. A rattlesnake bite was always bad, but to get bit down here in the gorge would be deadlier than a dose of the Flu.

Cecil's encounter with the snake had turned him around. His tracks were now facing back upstream. Watching every step—every stick and rock looked like a snake to me now—I followed the tracks up over a saddle and back down into the Garden Creek drainage, into the shadow of the Tonto Platform a thousand feet above me. It was getting late. Even if I found Cecil now, we wouldn't make it home before dark.

Crossing Garden Creek led me back to the lower stretches of Bright Angel Trail, two miles from the bridge. Several sets of mule tracks cluttered the trail. I couldn't tell whether Cecil had headed up or down. I decided to head back down. If Cecil had decided to head for the rim I wouldn't be able to catch him. Besides, I'd left my fish—and my sister—back at the river.

Darkness falls quickly in the canyon. Once the sun hits the rim, the shadows deepen, the temperature drops, and the sky turns to a deep indigo, like new blue jeans. Within minutes I was having trouble seeing. I picked my way carefully down the trail, still thinking about snakes. I stumbled several times on loose rocks and, at one point, skidded down a short slope on my butt. I had reached the river and was nearing the suspension bridge when I heard something between a chuckle and a snort—the sound a mule might make. Was it Cecil or Frosty? I stopped and listened, then heard the muted sound of hooves on sand, straight ahead. I continued forward, walking silently. The sun was gone, the moon had not yet risen, and the sky had turned from blue to dark slate. As I came around a grove of mesquite trees I saw Cecil standing beside the trail and, beside him, a human shape. For an instant I thought it was Harryette, but then I saw long, dark hair.

I said, "Hello?"

The figure turned toward me. I glimpsed wide eyes, smooth cheeks, the flash of white teeth.

"You found my mule," I said.

The figure stepped off the trail and melted into the dusk. My heart was pounding even harder than it had when I'd seen the rattlesnake. Rattlesnakes were dangerous, but they were a known danger.

Phantoms were something else entirely.

I found Harryette sitting on the sand spit by the rapids. She had started a small fire, and was roasting a trout on the end of a stick. The smell hit me right in the belly. I hadn't eaten in hours. I tied Cecil next to Frosty, doing a better job with the knots this time, and joined Harryette at the fire.

You found him.

I nodded.

Hungry?

Yes.

She handed me a second sharpened stick. I skewered a gutted trout and propped it up near the fire. We sat listening to the skin crackle and spit. Globs of trout fat fell into the fire, little firebombs making the flames dance higher.

I saw the Phantom, I signed.

Harryette shook her head. *You are a pain. Uncle is going to kill you.*

I saw it, really. If it wasn't a ghost, it was a person. A girl.

You were seeing things. Nobody lives in the canyon anymore.

Then it had to be the Phantom.

I'm not listening to you.

Why not? You believe in the Kinka. The Kinka, according to stories we had heard from travelers, were a band of marauding Survivors. It was said that wherever they appeared, they left behind only death.

The Kinka are real.

In your dreams, maybe.

Harryette shrugged. I could tell she was mad at me, but there was nothing I could do about it. We ate our fish without talking. It tasted great, even without salt. By the time we finished, the full moon had appeared over the rim.

We filled our water bags, loaded up the mules, and headed back up the trail by the light of the moon. We rode in silence, trusting Cecil and Frosty to stay on the trail. It reminded me of the trip Harryette and I had made after our parents had died. We had walked all the way from Williams to the canyon—eighty miles without talking. There had been no point in trying.

Harryette had lost her speech, and nothing I said made sense to her. A gulf wider than the Grand Canyon had opened between us. Later, even though we learned to speak in sign language, it was never the same. Harryette had one foot in some other world, a private place she permitted no one to enter. Not even me.

We reached the rim at sunrise. Uncle stood waiting at the trailhead, exhausted and worried. I braced myself for the lecture of a lifetime, but all he did was take a long, hard look at the both of us, then turn and walk away. I walked the mules to their corral, fed and watered them, then staggered up to my room. I was too tired to worry about Uncle, or about anything else. I don't even remember falling into bed.

EMORY

SOMETHING TICKLED MY NOSE: I snorted and flailed, moving from dreams into grogginess. I rolled onto my side, squeezing my eyes shut against the light. As I began to slip back into sleep's soft embrace, the tickling returned, this time way up inside my nostril. I slapped at my face with a leaden arm, hit myself in the nose hard enough to send a shock of pain across my cheeks. Someone laughed. I opened my eyes and sat up.

The room was bright with afternoon light. Tim Gordon stood above me, grinning, holding a long blade of grass between his thumb and forefinger.

"I got it up there a good three inches," he said.

I threw my pillow at him. He just laughed and let it bounce off his chest.

When I thought about Tim, I always thought about him just like that—laughing and grinning, long blond hair falling over his face, green eyes jumping.

He said, "Your unc says he's gonna beat you bloody and feed you to the coyotes."

"I don't care what he does." Uncle made a lot of threats, but he never actually hurt me. The lecture would be bad enough. I swung my legs over the edge of the bed. I was still wearing the same clothes I'd rode up in, reeking of mules and sweat.

"Harryette said you almost lost a mule."

"It was all her fault."

"That's not what she says. She says she had to follow you to the river to keep you out of trouble."

I looked away. The one thing I didn't like about Tim was the way he acted around my sister. He wouldn't come out and admit it, but he had a huge crush on Harryette.

"She told me you thought you saw a ghost."

I stood up. "I gotta get cleaned up."

"Well, hurry up. Your unc sent me to get you. We got a problem we gotta talk about. They're down in the lobby."

Uncle and Hap were sitting in the big leather chairs near the fireplace, looking at a map and talking quietly. Emory stood off to the side, beneath Bullwinkle's head, big brown hands clasped over his belt buckle, naked face slack, earth-colored eyes half-lidded. Yellow teeth showed between rubbery lips. He was so tall that it looked as if Bullwinkle was about to give his bald head a lick.

I couldn't tell if he was listening to Uncle and Hap, or just lost in his own little world. Every few seconds he would make a smacking sound with his thick lips. One time I heard Hap say Emory was smart like a mule. I think he meant the big Survivor was smarter than he looked. I wondered what he'd been like before the Flu. I wondered what he'd lost.

Harryette, curled up on the sofa, had her nose in a book, probably something Tim had brought her. Tim was practically illiterate, but he knew she liked to read, and he always brought her books. He was sitting on the floor with his back to the fire, watching her. It was pathetic. Harryette was four years older than Tim. As far as she was concerned he was just a squirrelly kid. The whole thing made me sick.

Uncle and Hap stopped talking and looked at me. Hap grinned, his sun-blasted features crinkling. He said, "Hello there, young man!"

"Hi, Hap."

"Hear you did some fishing!"

I shrugged. Uncle's face was blank.

Hap said, "And here I thought it was just my kid knew how to get his self in trouble." He looked at Tim, who was trying to hide a huge grin.

I said, "If Tim was with me we'd probably still be down there."

Nobody thought that was funny. Oh well. I sat down on the sofa next to Harryette, not because I particularly wanted to sit next to her, but to keep Tim from doing it.

"So, what's going on?" I asked.

Hap and Uncle looked at each other. Hap's smile disappeared.

He said, "Chandler and I were just talking about that." Chandler was Uncle's real name, but Hap was the only one who ever used it. "You notice anything about the river when you were down there?"

"It's pretty low."

"I bet it's damn near bone dry. You know those folks up there in Page?"

I nodded. Page was a town at the foot of Lake Powell, eighty miles upstream. I didn't know them personally, but last I'd heard there were about thirty people still living there in a fenced compound. It was a regular stop on Hap's trading route.

"Well," Hap said, "we were just up that way, and they're all dead. Every last one of 'em."

I felt the news like a kick in the gut.

"The Flu?" I asked.

Hap nodded. We all sat silently for a few seconds. This was bad news, but nothing we hadn't heard before. There'd been an outbreak down in Sedona the year before, and one in Winslow. There were still some people alive in Sedona, but Winslow had turned into another ghost town. The people in Page had been lucky for years. They had kept their little town fenced off and were notoriously unfriendly to travelers but, as Uncle drilled into us, no matter how careful you are, the Flu can still get you. It can come with a traveling stranger, or a stray dog, or a migrating duck.

Hap said, "We camped out at Bitter Springs for four

days after we found them, just to make sure none of us had caught the bug."

Uncle said, "Tell them about the dam."

Hap cleared his throat and shifted in his chair. "We're a little worried about that."

The Glen Canyon Dam, just a few miles from Page, had been built back in the late 1900s to generate electricity. The water that backed up behind it formed Lake Powell. Of course, the dam wasn't making much electricity anymore. Who would use it?

Uncle said, "We're *a lot* worried about that."

Hap nodded. "Ever since the Flu hit, the folks in Page have been working the dam, opening up the valve gates to control the level of the lake. Now that they're gone, there's nobody up there keeping an eye on things. The lake's pretty high. I figure they got sick while the gates were closed. That's why the river's so dry. The only water we're seeing here is coming off the Little Colorado River and a few of the creeks. But Lake Powell, behind the dam, is rising. It'll be coming over the top pretty soon."

Harryette made a series of signs. Hap looked to me to translate.

"She wants to know why that's a problem. The Hoover Dam has been overflowing for three years."

"The Hoover was made for that," Uncle said. "It was built with a sloping base that lets the water sort of slide down it. That thing will hold for a hundred years. But the Glen Canyon Dam wasn't designed to handle an overflow. You've seen little waterfalls in creek beds, right? You know how it gets kinda hollowed out behind the waterfall? That's what will happen up there. A few months—maybe weeks—the base of the dam will be undercut and the whole thing will give way. It might happen even sooner. A big storm system could do it, or a little earthquake. All nine hundred trillion gallons of water in Lake Powell dumped into the canyon at once. There'll be a wall of water a thousand feet high. Rip the guts right out of the canyon."

Harryette signed, *There's nobody down there. Why are you so worried?*

Uncle read her, then signed back clumsily, *It will rip the ecosystem right out of the canyon. And the water will keep going.* Out loud, he said, "It's like dominoes."

"That's right," said Hap. "The water will rush three hundred miles down the canyon and hit the Hoover Dam like God with a firehose. The Hoover gives way, the thousand trillion gallons in Lake Mead will go, too. The flood will blast through Laughlin and Lake Havasu and take out the Parker Dam, another hundred miles down river. There are people there—dozens of settlements. It won't stop till it hits the Gulf."

As he spoke, I translated for Harryette.

"Bottom line is, the Glen Canyon goes, a lot of plants, animals, and people get washed all the way down to the Sea of Cortez."

We all sat quietly. Hap pulled a bag of tobacco from his shirt pocket. He rolled a cigarette, then offered the bag to Uncle, who accepted it and rolled one for himself. I'd never seen Uncle smoke a cigarette before.

"The thing is," Uncle said slowly, smoke curling from his mouth, "we've got to go up there and try to open those sluice gates."

"How come you didn't do it while you were there?" I asked.

"Didn't know how," said Hap. "Your uncle here, he's the one knows his way around machinery. Chandler could fix a busted radiator with spit and mud."

It was true. Uncle had kept our truck and generator and all the other machines we needed going for years.

"That dam's a lot bigger than my Land Rover," Uncle said. "But I guess we've got to give it a whirl."

"When do we go?" I asked.

Uncle shook his head. "You and Tim and Harryette are staying here. We'll be gone four or five days, maybe. Somebody's got to keep the mules fed. Besides, no point in risking all of our skins."

"What d'you mean? It's not that dangerous, is it?"

Uncle shook his head slowly. "Tell him the rest of it, Hap."

When Hap and Tim and Emory had arrived at Page, they knew right away something was wrong. The gate in the chain-link fence surrounding the compound hung open, and the air stank of death. The first body they found was a child, half-eaten by coyotes and vultures. The second one was a bloated figure locked in a car, the windows fogged with condensed body fluids. They quickly backed away from the compound, horrified and fearful of the Flu. Circling the town at a good distance, they climbed to a rocky outcropping above the compound and, looking down, saw several other bodies scattered among the buildings.

"What do you think?" Hap asked Emory.

Emory shrugged his wide shoulders. "I think they got the sickness."

"I know that, you silly ass."

A coyote trotted across an open area. Tim raised his rifle to shoot it, but Hap pushed the barrel down.

"We don't know what we're dealing with, son."

For the next hour they waited, watching for signs of life. Other than the lone coyote, they saw nothing.

Hap said, "What do you say, Emory? You want to go have a look-see?" Because Emory was a Survivor, he could be exposed to the Flu without getting sick.

Wordlessly, Emory climbed down the rocks and scaled the chain-link fence. He was gone for thirty minutes. Just when Hap was considering going in after him, Emory appeared.

"Everybody dead," he reported.

Hap shook his head sadly. Emory's report was no surprise.

"Most of them tied up," Emory said.

"Tied up? What do you mean?"

Emory crossed his thick wrists. "Like with rope. They all tied up."

Hap took a deep breath, fearing the worst. "You see anything else? Anything unusual?"

Emory had stared back at him, then handed over a piece of paper.

Hap pulled a paper from his pocket and unfolded it. "This is what Emory found," he said. I looked at Emory, still standing silently beneath the stuffed moose head.

Harryette took the paper. I read over her shoulder.

These are the words of the Kinka.

The Divine has touched these people and judged them wanting. None have joined us. All have died.

We mourn their passing, but we Survive.

We feel their pain, but we Survive.

All who Survive are welcome to join us. This World is our World.

The Kinka have spoken.

I drew a ragged breath. "They're real," I said.

Hap nodded. "They're real, all right. And they brought the Flu to Page."

"We think they did it on purpose," Uncle said. "They infected everybody in Page, hoping to make more Survivors."

"I thought you couldn't get the Flu from Survivors," I said.

"We don't know how they did it," Uncle said. "There's been a rumor of these Kinka infecting other communities. They must have some way of transporting the virus, but we don't know how, or why they do it."

I looked toward Emory, but all I saw was Bullwinkle's hairy head. Emory was gone.

Harryette was staring at the paper with ferocious intensity, her fingers white from holding it so tight. Uncle got up from his chair and tried to take the paper from her, but Harryette wouldn't let go.

Just then, we heard the sound of an engine starting.

EIGHT DAYS

EMORY DID NOT RETURN THAT NIGHT.

Hap was furious. "That stupid Survivor don't know enough to get his shoes on the right feet, and here he's gone wandering off in my Jeep. That burns my ass, I swear it does!"

"You know where he's going," Uncle said.

We were all sitting around the big table in the kitchen eating breakfast. Harryette had gotten up early to make fresh tortillas and *chilaquile* sauce. She knew chilaquiles was Uncle's favorite breakfast. I can't say it was one of my personal favorites: slimy hunks of tortilla floating around in sweet, red, spicy sauce. Fortunately, Hap had brought ten pounds of real coffee beans with him. It was pre-Flu stuff, but it tasted fine to me. I loaded it up with powdered creamer and honey, and washed down the chilaquiles, no problem. Tim was shoveling down his second helping. Anything Harryette made was fine with him.

Hap said, "I know where he *thinks* he's going! He can go straight to hell for all I care."

I asked, "You think he'll find them?"

"That boy's so stupid he's lucky to find his mouth with a chunk of food. Besides, the Kinka are probably halfway to Albuquerque by now."

Uncle loaded a forkful of chilaquiles into his mouth and chewed thoughtfully. Harryette, sitting across from me, signed, *What's he saying?*

Hap was telling Uncle that Emory is an idiot.

Harryette frowned. *He's not so stupid.*

I wasn't sure whether she was talking about Emory, Hap, or Uncle.

Uncle said, "None of that changes what we have to do."

"I know that," said Hap. "Damned if I don't know that. But I can't say I won't miss that bald-headed dolt."

Harryette signed, *I'm going with you.*

Uncle either didn't see her, or chose to ignore her. Harryette kicked me under the table and made an angry sign at me. *Tell him.*

I said, "Harryette wants to go."

Uncle and Hap both looked at me, then at Harryette.

You need me, she signed.

Uncle shook his head.

You can't go without a Survivor. Too dangerous.

"What's she saying?" Hap asked.

"She says you need her," I said.

Uncle shook his head harder. They glared at each other. I'd seen Uncle and Harryette lock horns plenty of times. There wasn't much question who was going to win.

Hap said, "You know, she's got a point, Chandler."

Uncle turned his fierce glare upon Hap.

"We might need her to go into Page. Also, if we run into those crazies—God forbid—we might need her to talk to 'em."

"She doesn't talk," said Uncle.

"You know what I mean. She can write and sign."

Uncle looked at Harryette.

I'm going with you, she signed.

Early the next morning Tim and I watched them leave—Hap, Uncle, and Harryette in the Land Rover. I felt afraid for them. But mostly I was angry about being left behind. As the rear end of the Land Rover disappeared behind the wall of pine trees, Tim said, "What do you want to do?"

I didn't know what I wanted to do, but I knew what I *had* to do. "Let's clean up the breakfast dishes. Then I got to set up the perimeter alarms, then brush down and feed Cecil and Frosty."

"You want to go fishing instead?"

"Shut up."

"Want to go hunting?"

"We've got plenty of meat. Uncle shot a prong-horn last week."

Tim followed me back into the hotel. While I gathered the dishes and began to wash them, he "helped" me by keeping up a steady chatter. For a few minutes he talked about a group of travelers he and Hap had seen heading west on I-40 near Flagstaff.

"They were like these robot people, marching down the middle of the freeway. They had uniforms. There were about a hundred of them. Wearing these black and green uniforms and big blue backpacks and marching like to music, but there wasn't any."

"You think they were the Kinka?"

"Nah. Kinkas are all Survivors. This bunch had hair. They were some other sort of cult. You should come with us next time we drive our circuit. We see all kinds of cool stuff. One time we visited this bunch of naked people down by Sedona. Called themselves 'Naturists.' We traded them a case of sunblock for some dried beef."

"You told me about that." Actually, he'd told me about the Naturists about six times.

"There was this one looked kind of like Sigourney Weaver."

That's how weird Tim was. He had watched all of the *Alien* movies twice. He thought Sigourney Weaver was the most beautiful woman who ever lived.

"I'm not sitting through *Alien* again," I said.

"So what do you want to do?"

"Finish these dishes, set up the perimeter alarms, brush down the mules."

Tim rolled his eyes. After a moment he said, "You should've seen the one in the car."

"Are we talking about the Naturists?"

"No. I mean in Page. The windows were all foggy but you could see the guy's face. It was like his eyes had popped out. And then the wind shifted and the smell hit us. I puked, just like that." He looked like he was going to puke again, just thinking about it.

"I wish we'd gone with them," I said.

"Not me," said Tim.

The perimeter alarms were basically wires strung a couple of inches above the ground. If somebody tripped on one, it would set off a battery-operated horn. Uncle had salvaged the horns and batteries from old cars. We had alarms on all the roads and foot trails leading into the village. Usually we didn't bother with them because it took forever to set them up, and they were as likely to be triggered by a deer as anything. But Uncle had made me promise, so Tim and I spent the next two hours testing batteries, stringing trip wires and camouflaging them with sticks and leaves.

Of course, when you do something with Tim, it's never ordinary. I was bent over one of the horns attaching a wire when I felt a buzz in my fingertips and the thing went off right in my ear. I was so startled I fell over backwards.

Tim was laughing so hard I thought he'd choke, but he must have been breathing okay because I chased him all the way around Hopi House twice before giving up. I went back to stringing the alarms. My ears were still ringing.

Tim showed his face when I was about finished. He said he was sorry. Tim wasn't very good at apologizing. He must've about bit his tongue off trying not to laugh. I used his contrite mood, such as it was, to ask him to take care of the mules. Grudgingly, he agreed.

As soon as Tim was out of sight, I took a battery, some lamp cord, and the biggest horn I had—I think it was from a Mack truck—and carried it up to his bedroom. I hid the horn under the head of his bed, then ran the wires under the edge of the carpet and down the hall to my room. All I had to do was wait till he was asleep, touch the wires to the poles of the battery, and send him right through the roof.

That night, after a dinner of pronghorn steaks, tortillas, and canned artichoke hearts, we put on a disc and watched *Ghostbusters,* another of Tim's favorites. We'd both seen it at least three times before. I suppose it was stupid of us to watch it again, since there were about a thousand other movies in Uncle's collection. I guess we needed to see something familiar. We didn't talk about Uncle and Harryette and Hap. We didn't want to think about it. I wanted to watch the Ghostbusters bust ghosts, and Tim wanted to watch Sigour-ney Weaver possessed by demons. We were at the part where Dan Ackroyd gets slimed when the picture flickered, came back, then died completely. The room went black.

Tim said, "Hey!"

I groaned. "It's the generator."

"It broke?"

"No, I just have to switch over to the other tank."

"Well, hurry up!" Tim could be pretty selfish.

I felt my way out of the room, found the flashlight by the kitchen door, and walked out back to the generator shed.

The gasoline that ran our generator was stored in two eighty-gallon tanks behind the shed. Every few weeks, Uncle and I would load the empty tanks onto a trailer, drive down to Tusayan, and pump them full from the Texaco station. Uncle figured there was enough gas there to last us another five or six years. After that, we would have to drive all the way to Flagstaff for our fuel.

Checking the gauge on the left tank, I saw that it was completely empty, as I expected. I closed the petcock, then opened the one on the other tank. While I was doing this I kept an eye out for Tim. It would be just like him to follow me, then jump out from the dark. I didn't need any of that right then—just going into that shed was scary enough. I had once walked in on a rattler, and there was almost always a black widow or two hanging out. I opened the door and stepped back. With the beam of the flashlight, I explored the dirt floor of the shed. No snakes, tarantulas, gila monsters, or other poisonous, crawling critters. I raised the light and checked the walls and corners. I saw a couple of widows, but they were safely tucked into their ragged webs. I stepped in and pressed the starter on the generator.

It rumbled to life. Excellent. I backed out of the shed and instantly felt something grip and dig into my left calf. I yelped and jumped away.

"Gotcha," said Tim.

I threw the flashlight at him. He ducked, laughing, as the flashlight hit a rock and went out.

"Now you did it," he said.

We picked our way back to the lodge in the dark.

"I'm gonna get you good," I promised.

We watched the rest of *Ghostbusters,* then went to bed. I laid awake for an hour and a half, until I was sure that Tim was deep asleep. Then I turned on my light, untaped the ends of the wire that led to the Mack truck horn, and touched them to the battery.

The sound of the truck horn shook the walls. I could almost see Tim blasted from a dead sleep—I bet he jumped three feet off the mattress, every nerve in his body screaming.

When he came charging through the door to my room a minute later I was laughing so hard I didn't even mind the bucket of water he dumped on me.

Tim and I always had a good time together.

After a couple days we both calmed down and quit playing jokes on each other. Actually, it got pretty boring. The perimeter alarm was tripped on the second night, and we both scrambled out of bed and took up our defense positions, but it turned out to be nothing. Probably just a deer, or a bear. In the morning I woke up holding my rifle, still sitting guard at the window.

The next day we hiked to the outlook at Yavapai Point. From there, we could see a small section of river, and most of Phantom Ranch. I pointed out some of the other landmarks, showing off a bit.

"That pointed butte over there, like a mountain, that's called Isis Temple, and behind it, with the flat top, that's Shiva Temple. And just to the right of that is Cheops Pyramid."

"How come they got all those weird names?"

"I guess the first explorers that got here named them. I mean, the Indians were here first, and they probably gave them other names, but the ones I know are the ones in English." I pointed out Zoroaster Temple, Angel's Gate, Wotan's Throne.

"Who's Wotan?"

"Some really big guy, I guess."

"How come you know all these names?"

"Uncle," I said. Harryette and I didn't go to school. There were no schools. But Uncle had taught us everything he knew. There wasn't a peak or canyon or bird or plant within ten miles that I didn't know the name of.

"When you went down to the river, did you always know where you were?"

"Sure I did. The trail's still in pretty good shape. It's

hard to get lost completely down there, since you always know you're between the river and the rim, and which way's up.

Tim shook his head. "I could get lost."

As I stared into the vastness that lay before us, I suddenly felt my heart begin to pound. I had gotten used to living on the rim. But every now and then I would look down into it and the size and beauty of it would suck the breath right out of my lungs. This wasn't just a slash in the earth. I knew in that moment why those early explorers had given these buttes names like Apollo Temple, Angel's Gate, and Tower of Ra. There was something holy in this place. Something terrifying and powerful and sacred and awesome, and whatever it was had touched me yet again.

Tim said, "Are you okay?"

I nodded wordlessly, swimming in a sense of wonder.

On the fourth day I started to worry.

"What if something happened?" I said.

Tim bent over and picked up a rock. "They're probably on their way back." He threw the stone out into the abyss. "Maybe they're having truck problems."

I wanted to believe that, but I had a bad feeling. Looking through Uncle's spotting scope, I could see that the river was drier than ever. If Uncle and Hap had succeeded in opening the gates, we should have seen the water rise.

"Maybe something happened," I said.

Tim gave me a dark look and walked away.

The next morning I got up and walked out to the rim and looked down on the river. It looked different. I went back inside and got the scope and looked again. It was definitely wider. I ran to wake up Tim.

"They did it!"

Tim was pretty foggy. "Did what?"

"The river is up. They must've got the gates open."

He sat up, scratching his head. "They did?" His face broke into a grin.

We celebrated by having eggs and venison sausage for breakfast. It was a wonderful feeling knowing that Uncle and Hap had succeeded in changing the way the river ran—the same river that had carved out this enormous canyon, slicing a mile deep into the earth. They had made it flow again.

Our feeling of euphoria lasted through that day, and through the next, when we expected the Land Rover to come rumbling down the East Rim Drive. I spent the whole day waiting for the blare of the perimeter alarm.

Two days later, we were still waiting.

INTO THE ABYSS

ON THE NINTH DAY, Tim and I loaded up the mules. We packed enough food and water to last us for two weeks. That was how long it would take us to get to Page and back. Of course, we hoped we wouldn't get that far. We hoped we would run into Uncle and Hap and Harryette along the way. They would be furious with us for not waiting. It would be a pleasure to listen to Uncle rant and rave. I even missed Harryette's smirking face.

The first day, we planned to make it to the Desert View Watchtower, the stone tower near the east entrance to the park. From the top of the seventy-foot-tall tower we would be able to see for a hundred miles. Maybe we would be able to spot them. If not, we would continue on Highway 64, through Cameron, then north to Hidden Springs, and eventually to Page. It should have been an exciting journey, but as we left Grand Canyon Village I was overwhelmed by a sense of dread. I held the reins with one hand, and kept my other resting lightly on the stock of the 30-30 carbine in my saddle holster.

Tim, riding a few yards behind me, kept up a steady stream of chatter. I could tell he was nervous, too. Every few seconds he would reach back and touch the shotgun strapped to the back of his saddle. After the first few miles, the clop of mule hoofs on the crumbling tarmac, regular as a metronome, lulled me into a daze. The trees marched slowly by, and white clouds boiled in the sky above. We had been traveling for two hours when Tim pulled up beside me.

"What?"

"Stop!"

We reined in the mules.

"Listen."

I heard the breeze in the trees, and Cecil's breathing. Then I heard the sound of an engine, growing louder.

"It's the Land Rover," said Tim.

An instant later, the Land Rover came into view a quarter mile ahead. I waved. The engine sound quieted, and it braked to a stop a hundred yards in front of us. I gave the reins a shake, urging Cecil forward.

"Hold up," said Tim. "Something's wrong."

We could see only one person in the Land Rover—the driver.

"Is it Hap?" I asked.

"It's not Hap."

The Land Rover jerked and started forward.

"It's not Uncle," I said as the shape of the driver's head became clear.

"It's somebody else. Come on." Tim gave Frosty a kick and headed off the road, away from the rim and into the trees. I waited, still trying to make out the features of the approaching driver. He was bald, like Emory and Harryette, but his face was painted pale yellow, and his eyes were outlined with red. Suddenly the engine roared and the Land Rover hurtled toward me. I jerked the reins to the side and gave Cecil a kick in the flanks. He reared, then bolted. The Land Rover roared past, missing his flank by inches. Cecil galloped into the woods, nearly taking my head off on a low tree branch. I hunched low in the saddle and followed Tim, who was zigzagging his way through the trees. Behind me, I could hear the angry honking of the Land Rover's horn.

I caught up with Tim a few minutes later in a dry, rocky creek bed. He was sitting on his mule, his face white, holding his shotgun in shaking hands. I probably looked worse. I sure felt worse.

"Watch where you point that thing."

"They got 'em," he said, moving the barrel away. "The Kinka got 'em."

"We don't know that for sure."

"They got the Land Rover."

"Maybe Uncle traded it to them. Or they just stole it."

Tim shook his head.

"What are we going to do?" I said. "If we go back to the village they'll find us there."

Tim dismounted and sat down on a lichen-covered rock. "They'll get us next."

"No. We can hide until they leave." I climbed down off Cecil and sat beside him. "I know these woods. They won't find us if we don't want them to."

Tim shook his head. "That stupid dam. All because of a stupid dam."

In the distance, I heard honking.

I said, "Look, they might be okay. Maybe they got away and are hiding like us, just waiting until the Kinka move on. Uncle and Hap know how to take care of themselves. And you know Harryette—she's practically bulletproof."

Tim nodded. He wanted to believe me. I wanted to believe me, too. It frightened me to see Tim so scared, but it helped, too. Seeing him that messed up, I knew I had to be the strong one.

"We have to get farther away," I said.

"Away from *where?* We don't even know where they *are!* We don't even know how many. There might be a thousand of them."

"Or there might only be one or two." I stood up and took Cecil's reins. "Come on," I said. "We'll walk the mules up the creek. They won't be able to track us over all these rocks. I know where there's an old cabin we can stay in." I started off.

Woodenly, Tim rose to his feet and followed. We walked a half mile up the creek, lost in our own thoughts and fears. At the collapsed bridge, we climbed out of the creek bed and followed an old jeep trail south until we reached a dilapidated cabin I had discovered the previous summer.

"We can stay here."

Tim looked through the cobwebbed doorway at the trash-strewn interior. "Nice place."

I half-smiled. At least he still had his sense of humor. We sat outside the cabin and ate a cold lunch of pronghorn jerky and canned pears. The woods were still and windless. Tiny flies hovered around our heads; the carpet of pine needles absorbed the sound of their buzzing. As our bellies filled, the Kinka seemed less real. Maybe it wasn't the Kinka at all. Maybe some crazy lone Survivor had stolen the Land Rover.

Tim said, "You know what we gotta do, don't you?"

I looked up.

"We gotta go back. We gotta go find out where they're camped. If they got my dad and your uncle and Harryette, maybe we can do something." He ran his hand up and down the barrel of his shotgun. "Maybe we can save them."

We left the cabin at sunset and led the mules northeast through the forest, paralleling the rim drive. It was slow going at first, but once the moon rose we were able to move easily through the trees. Years ago, a forest fire had burned up part of the forest. Blackened tree trunks stood among the young trees like silent dark sentinels. That night they looked to me like Kinka. Every few minutes we stopped and listened, but heard only the faint sounds of small animals and the gentle night breeze passing though the trees.

I had an idea about where the Kinka—if it *was* the Kinka—might be camped. There was an overlook a mile up-canyon called Moran Point. It was a natural stopping place and a good spot to camp. Even a group of crazy Survivors would appreciate the view.

An hour of slow, careful walking brought us to an overgrown jeep trail. We stopped again and listened, but heard nothing.

"This takes us back to the rim road," I said. "We'll come out opposite of Moran Point."

Tim nodded, his face bright with moonlight. We followed the trail, listening to the soft crunch of mule hooves on twigs and pine needles. We stopped every few yards to listen. When we reached the rim drive I suggested that we park the mules and go in on foot. We crossed the road and left the mules in the woods between the road and the rim.

Proceeding on foot, we walked the quarter mile to the Moran Point access road. Again, we stopped and listened. But this time it was not Tim's ears that alerted us, it was my nose.

"I smell smoke," I whispered.

Tim sniffed the air. "Me, too." The breeze was coming from the canyon. "You were right. They're camped at the point."

"We have to get closer, find out how many of them there are."

We crossed the access road and made our way through the woods between the rim drive and the rim itself. It was only a couple hundred yards. The canyon in moonlight was a beautiful sight, but neither of us was in a mood to appreciate it. We worked our way along the rocky edge slowly, until we reached the edge of the small loop drive. We crouched behind a fallen tree. The glow of a campfire showed through a grove of junipers and pinyon pine at the center of the loop. The mutter of voices filtered through the trees. They were camped right at the overlook, fifty yards away. We couldn't see them clearly, only momentary glimpses of firelight reflecting off hairless heads.

"It's them," I whispered.

To get any closer we would have to cross the loop road. If they had any guards posted, or if one of them just happened to wander away from the fire, we might be seen.

Tim said, "I can make it to those trees. They won't see me." He crept forward, then made a dash across the loop road and disappeared into a copse of junipers. I sucked in my breath and held it. There was no shouting or shooting or sudden silence. The voices continued to mumble, with an occasional burst of laughter. He'd made it! I let my breath out. My heart was banging around in my chest like a packrat in a trap. What was he seeing? I wished I'd gone with him, but I was too scared to move. Five or ten minutes passed, but it seemed like hours. What was he doing? A shadow appeared to the left of the trees; moonlight glanced off a naked skull. A Kinka was walking down the center of the road, coming in my direction. I ducked down behind the fallen tree and watched him through a screen of dry pine needles. When he was only a few yards away, he stopped and unzipped his pants. Urine splashed on tarmac; a few seconds later I could smell it. The Survivor zipped up, then ambled slowly back toward the campfire. I swallowed, trying to moisten my dry throat.

That was when everything happened. There was a shout, then excited voices. I saw bald heads in motion, then Tim burst from the junipers, his legs pumping, heading right at me. He hurdled the fallen tree and kept right on going.

"Run!" he shouted over his shoulder.

I didn't need to be told twice. I took off after him, running at top speed in the dark, branches tearing at us, rocks and logs trying to trip us at every stride. It felt like we'd been running forever, but it couldn't have taken more than a few minutes for us to reach the mules. I untied Cecil and leapt onto his back. He snorted and stamped his feet in protest. Instead of reassuring him, I gave Cecil a kick in the flanks like he'd never gotten before. He got the message, launching himself forward. Keeping my head low, my cheek pressed to the side of his neck, I guided him out of the

woods onto the rim drive and headed west. Tim and
Frosty were right behind us. I heard the sound of an
engine and gave Cecil another kick, urging him to a full
gallop. We pounded down the road. Tim shouted
something. I couldn't hear his words through the clatter of hooves, the rasping of breath, and the thudding
of my pulse, but I knew he was telling me to head off
into the woods. I made a scooping motion with my
arm, telling him to keep following me. Headlights
appeared behind us. I strained to see what lay ahead. I
was looking for an open spot on the right side of the
road, a place marked with a few stubby posts and an
old sign. It had to be close. Tim came up beside me,
pointing urgently at the woods to our left. I shook my
head. We were almost there. There! I pulled back on
the reins. Cecil snorted and stopped, I turned him
back, then headed him between two wooden posts and
onto an overgrown trail leading toward the canyon.

"We'll be trapped between the road and the rim,"
Tim shouted from the road.

"No we won't!" I yelled back.

Tim hesitated. The roar of the engine—two
engines—got louder. Headlights washed across him.
He would come, or he wouldn't. I headed toward the
rim, pushing Cecil as fast as he would go, hoping that
Tim was right behind me. I didn't look back until Cecil
came to an abrupt halt where the trail suddenly
dropped into a steep switchback. The moonlit canyon
spread out before us.

I heard Frosty's hooves coming up, and Tim's voice saying, "I hope you know what you're doing."

We could hear engines racing, and see flashes of light coming through the trees.

"So do I," I said. I urged Cecil forward. "We're going down."

RED CANYON

IT HAD BEEN A WHILE SINCE I'd explored the trail into Red Canyon, and it had been in rough shape back then. I hoped that it hadn't washed out completely. Even when it had been in good shape, the Red Canyon Trail was one of the steepest, most treacherous ways to get into the canyon. Going down it at night, on mules, was practically insane.

Cecil didn't want to enter the first switchback. I didn't blame him. I leaned close to his long ear and said, "Apple, Cecil. Let's go!" Reluctantly, he headed down the steep, rocky trail, placing his hooves carefully. I sat lightly on his back, trying to make it as easy for him as I could. Once a mule gets going on a canyon trail, it's not a good idea to distract it—one small misstep could prove deadly.

I looked back. Tim was right there, hanging onto Frosty, looking terrified.

"Just let Frosty do the work," I said.

He nodded.

We were only a hundred feet down the trail when the Kinka reached the rim. I heard shouting, then the clatter of feet on rocks. One of them cried, "Wait, come back!" I wasn't sure whether they were calling to us, or to one of their own. "We won't hurt you," the voice said.

"Keep on moving, buddy," I said in Cecil's ear. To our left was a steep talus slope—a sloping field of rubble—that ended forty feet below me in a sheer cliff.

I heard a grunt of surprise and turned to see Tim struggling, flailing with his fists. One of the Kinka had caught up and was trying to pull him off the mule. Frosty danced on the narrow section of trail as Tim struck at the Kinka. I pulled my rifle from the saddle holster and tried to aim, but in the dark, with the two of them so close, I couldn't risk a shot. Then Tim had his shotgun out. He swung it like a club, hitting the Kinka on the ear. The Kinka howled, staggered back, lost his footing and tumbled down the talus slope. For a moment I thought he would catch himself on one of the small, shrubby trees that dotted the slope, but the Kinka just kept rolling until he disappeared over the edge of the cliff. Judging by the length of his scream, he must have dropped a couple hundred feet before he hit.

Tim sat unmoving on Frosty, staring after the Kinka. I reholstered my rifle.

"We have to keep moving," I said.

Tim nodded. We continued down, looking back every few seconds. We could still hear the voices, now a hundred feet above us. For almost a minute, nothing happened.

Then the rocks began to fall. The first rocks were small—we couldn't see them, but we heard them hitting behind us, rolling down the slopes and causing mini-avalanches. Above us, the Kinka were shouting and laughing. Then they started to push the big rocks down on us. I heard a loud crunching, ripping sound from above us. A boulder as big as an easy chair smashed through a juniper and plowed across the trail a few feet in front of me. Cecil reared. Several smaller rocks, dislodged by the boulder, came skidding and bouncing in its wake. One of them glanced off my shoulder, nearly knocking me off. Cecil suddenly bolted forward, and another huge boulder came thumping down, end-over-end, right behind us. I heard Tim shout and turned just in time to see a rock the size of a loaf of bread hit Frosty on the side of the head. The mule collapsed instantly, throwing Tim forward onto her neck. She tried to right herself, but the edge of the trail, damaged by falling rock, gave way. They began to slide, unable to stop themselves on the loose scree. I lost sight of Tim. Frosty let loose a horrific squeal as she went over the edge into the drainage. I saw a flash of white—Tim's face? Had he gone over? From directly above, I heard another boulder coming. I dug my heels into Cecil's flanks, sending us down the trail at a dangerous clip. Within seconds we reached the protection of a limestone overhang. I dismounted and listened as more boulders came crashing down from the rim, the echoes of their descent swallowed up by the vastness of the canyon. After a few minutes, the bombardment stopped. I grabbed my rifle and began to walk quietly back up the trail, ready to shoot anything that moved. At the spot where Frosty and Tim had been knocked off the trail, I stopped. I couldn't see either of them. The steep slope beside the trail was dotted with scrub oak and agaves. Forty feet down, the slope ended in a precipice that could have been five feet—or five hundred feet. I stood and listened. I wanted desperately to call out for Tim, but I was afraid that if the Kinka heard me the rocks would come again. I waited for some sign that he had survived—a groan of pain, anything—but I heard nothing. Even the Kinka were silent. Either they had gotten bored and left, or they were creeping down the trail—or they were waiting, like me, for a sound. I considered scrambling down the slope to look over the edge—there were enough plants and rocks to grab onto—but I was afraid the Kinka would hear me and send another barrage of rocks. I decided to continue down the trail a few hundred yards, then bushwhack my way back up the drainage. Maybe I could reach them from below.

As I approached the overhang where I'd left Cecil, I heard a low voice. How could they have gotten in front of me? I moved forward slowly. I saw Cecil first, then a figure standing beside him, talking in his ear. I raised the rifle to my shoulder.

"Don't move," I said.

The figure turned toward me.

"I was afraid they got you," said Tim.

The precipice Tim and Frosty had tumbled over was only about twenty feet high. Tim had landed directly on top of Frosty, then bounced into a tangle of wolfberry bushes. He was pretty scratched up.

"You're sure she's dead?" I'd known Frosty most of my life.

"I think the rock that hit her did it."

Tim had salvaged what he could from the saddle-bags. His shotgun hadn't survived the fall, and both water jugs had burst upon impact, but he'd been able to save some food, a blanket, and a few other odds and ends. He had loaded it all into the shell of the nylon tent and, using the tent as a sack, made his way down the narrow ravine, looking for a place to climb out. At a place where the side of the drainage had collapsed he had been able to scramble up a pile of broken boulders and, after stumbling around in the dark for a while, he had found the trail.

"We better keep moving," I said. We tied the remains of Tim's packs onto Cecil's saddle. We would all be walking now. I started down, leading Cecil, and Tim brought up the rear. Tim had my rifle—if we were attacked again, it would come from behind.

We picked our way down the steep, rocky trail, waiting for more rocks to fall, or for a band of Kinka to come swarming upon us. Intent on listening, we did not talk.

An hour of slow walking—the trail became more treacherous with every step—brought us to the Coconino sandstone layer, an area dotted by junipers and enormous boulders. We stopped there and sat down on a flat rock looking out over Red Canyon. I pulled a bag of roasted pine nuts from my pocket and offered some to Tim. We sat munching and looking down into the gorge. In the moonlight, we could see the Redwall, the sheer, six-hundred-foot-high lime-stone cliff that ran the entire length of the canyon, waiting a quarter of a mile below us. The Redwall is the most precipitous part of the canyon. Except for a few dozen established trails through breaks in the Redwall, traversing it on foot is impossible. The Red Canyon trail would take us down, but it would not be easy.

Tim said, "So, you want to know what I saw?"

My heart jumped in my chest; followed by a wave of nausea. I'd been so busy thinking about our imme-diate danger, about where my next footfall should go, that I'd blocked out the reason we'd visited the Kinka camp in the first place.

"What," I said, dreading what I was about to hear.

"There were about forty of 'em," Tim said. "They were drinking something. Some kind of liquor. Sitting around the fire. Actually, only about a dozen of them were drinking. A lot of them were just sitting there looking vacant. You know, like Emory. He was one of them, by the way. He's got paint all over his face now. They all had paint on their heads. They were mostly men, a few women, and a few little kids. It was one of the kids that spotted me and started hollering."

"It's a good thing they were drunk," I said. "Otherwise they might've got us."

Tim held out his hand for more nuts. I poured a few more into his hand.

"One of the women seemed to be in charge," he continued. "I got a good look at her. She was black—or maybe she was painted black, and she was wearing tons of jewelry. Gold chains and earrings and bracelets—everything. She jangled when she walked, and she had these light colored eyes, kind of gold colored. Everybody called her Mother K, but I don't think she was really anybody's mother. She was walking around putting her hand on people's heads, or she would shout at one of them to put another log on the fire or help with the cooking. She was the one that started yelling orders when that little kid spotted me."

Tim took another handful of nuts.

"Did you see Hap?" I was afraid to ask about Uncle and Harryette.

Tim shook his head. "No, but they have the Land Rover and the Jeep and a big old bus—like a school bus? There were some people inside. They could've been in there."

After a few seconds of chewing, Tim said, "There's

something else. The one they called Mother K, I saw her talking to this one girl. I couldn't see them too good—they were on the other side of the fire—and they weren't talking, actually. They were writing things in the dirt with a stick."

"Why were they doing that?" I asked, even though I knew the answer.

"I'm pretty sure it was Harryette."

"You think she's their prisoner?"

"She wasn't tied up or anything."

"We have to go get her," I said. "Hap and Uncle, too."

"If they're there."

"Harryette wouldn't just leave Uncle and Hap. She's not like Emory. And she wouldn't join up with a bunch like that. She wouldn't have let them roll rocks down on us."

"Maybe she's the one that stopped them," Tim said.

I loaded the water jug back in the saddlebag. "Whatever, we have to find out."

"You're not thinking of going back up the trail, are you?"

"No way. They'd be up there waiting for us. We'll hike down to the river, then come back up a different way. There are lots of ways to get in and out of the canyon. It might take us a couple days, but when we make it back to the rim they won't know where to expect us."

"What if they're gone?"

"We'll find them." I grasped Cecil's reins. "Let's get moving."

Dawn found us picking our way through the Redwall layer, where the switchbacks were steep and the trail narrow. I had hoped the daylight would make the going easier, but now that we could see what we were walking on, I was doubly nervous. The trail was completely washed out in places, forcing us to scramble across steep talus slopes and climb over unstable piles of boulders. Twice I stepped on a loose bit of scree and nearly went down. Even Cecil seemed uncertain and fearful.

We reached the bottom of the Redwall in a state of nervous exhaustion. My legs ached, and my mind had retreated. I felt like I was looking out of my skull through eye-shaped windows. Vishnu Temple, a majestic butte on the north side of the canyon, rose directly in front of us, its pointed summit glowing in the morning sun. Deep inside myself I recognized its beauty, but I felt nothing but weariness. We were still two thousand feet above the river.

"We should stop," I said. "If we keep going, one of us is going to get hurt. My legs feel like rubber."

We rested in the shade of the Redwall, watching the colors of the canyon change as the sun rose higher, lighting more of Vishnu Temple, then Rama Shrine, then the dozens of smaller, nameless buttes. Far to the west

I could see Angel's Gate jutting up like the roots of an oversize molar, and the enormous, detached section of rim known as Wotan's Throne. A few yards in front of us a grizzly bear cactus displayed three brilliant pink flowers. Next to that was the stump of a yucca plant, its leaves gnawed off, possibly by a desert tortoise. If I'd been less exhausted I would have pointed these things out to Tim. As it was I simply noted them to myself.

At some point I fell asleep. When I awakened, the sun was directly above us. Tim was standing a few yards off the trail looking at something.

"What do you see?" I asked.

"Some kind of big lizard."

I stood up, my legs complaining, and looked where he was pointing. A fat, gray-green lizard more than two feet long was sunning itself on a flat rock.

"That's a chuckwalla," I said. "If we run out of food, we might have to eat one."

"I don't plan to get that hungry," Tim said.

"You never know."

The chuckwalla, perhaps understanding something of our conversation, scurried off. We laughed for the first time in more than a day.

"You ready to go?" I asked.

Tim nodded.

We lost the trail several times, but were able to find it by searching for cairns, small piles of rocks that hikers had used years ago to mark the way down. It took us another four hours to reach the river.

Two Small Holes

WE MADE CAMP IN A MESQUITE grove above a small rapids.
Setting up the tent was a problem——Frosty had landed
on top of the tent poles, and the few that Tim had been
able to salvage weren't good for much. We made do by
tying the top of the tent to a mesquite branch above
us. After a makeshift meal of crackers, sardines, and
jerky, I took our water jug down to the river to fill it.

The water was high, and the rapids were roaring. I
followed the shoreline upstream to a spot where I
could dip the jugs into a pool. To my surprise, the
water was warm. In the past, every time I'd been to
the river, especially when it was high, the water had
been icy cold. Just washing my hands in it would leave
my fingers numb. But this water was warm enough to
swim in.

I filled the jug, added a purification tablet, and
trudged back toward camp. The sun had dropped
below the rim; the canyon was in shadow. High above,
wisps of cloud stood out against deep blue. I saw an
enormous black bird about fifty feet above me, sailing
down canyon, too big to be a hawk or an eagle. I was

looking at a California condor. When I was born they had been all but extinct. Now, with most of the humans on the planet dead, the condors were coming back. Maybe the six billion dead humans had been the edge they needed. At least one good thing had come out of the Flu.

I'd seen condors before, but never this close. I watched the giant bird sailing down the gorge until it caught a thermal—a channel of warm, rising air—and spiraled up a few thousand feet. As it left the shadow of the canyon walls, sunlight glanced from its naked pink head. With ponderous grace, the great bird banked and glided off toward Wotan's Throne.

Still looking up, I took a step forward. My foot landed on a rock and skidded off. Weighed down by the water jug, I staggered to the side, stepping into a tangle of driftwood, almost falling. Something slapped against my ankle, causing a sharp pain. Cursing, I extracted myself from the pile of twisted branches, and kept moving toward camp, watching my footfalls. I could have twisted my ankle, or worse, but it seemed to be okay. I reminded myself to be careful. If something happened, we were on our own.

By the time I reached camp the temperature had dropped. I was glad to see that Tim had built a small fire. Cecil was grazing on a patch of grass down near the rapids.

"I saw a condor," I said, dropping down to sit beside him.

Tim nodded, poking the fire with a stick. "That's a big vulture, right?"

"Yeah, their wings are ten feet across."

"Let's just hope we don't see one face to face."

"The only way that would happen is if we were dead and it was eating us."

"That's what I mean." He tossed more wood on the fire. My ankle was throbbing. I reached down to massage it. It didn't feel twisted, but it didn't feel right, either.

"What's the matter?" Tim asked.

"I hit my ankle on something."

"You okay?"

"Yeah." We sat listening to the crackle of burning mesquite, the peeping of frogs, the rushing rapids.

Tim said, "This is the worst day of my life."

I couldn't argue. We'd lost a mule, we'd lost our families, and we were stuck at the bottom of the biggest hole on the planet.

"Let's get some sleep," I said, standing up. My right foot felt like it was made of lead. A sharp pain rocketed up my calf. I gasped and sat back down.

"You okay?"

"I'm not sure." I untied my hiking boot and pulled it off. Released from the boot, my foot felt better, but only for a moment. I peeled off my sock.

"You must've twisted it good. It's all swollen."

I stared at the ankle, reached down and touched it gingerly. Something there—a red lump just above the anklebone. I leaned closer. A shaft of fear pierced my abdomen.

I heard Tim's voice, as if from a distance. "Jeez, what did you do?"

I didn't answer. I was staring at two tiny puncture wounds, angry red eyes, about three quarters of an inch apart.

"I think I got bit," I said.

I knew what to do. Uncle had drilled us in snakebite treatment. The instructions were frighteningly simple: Cut, suck, rest, and hope.

Tim used his knife to make two short, shallow cuts, one over each fang mark. It hurt, but I was too scared to care. He sucked and spat, trying to draw the poison out of the wound. I didn't figure it would do much good, since almost half an hour had passed since I was bit, but we did it anyway. After about ten minutes I told him to stop. By that time I was feeling a lot worse. My entire leg was pulsing with sharp, electric bolts of pain. My tongue felt thick, and I was sweating gallons.

"I'm gonna be okay," I said.

Tim handed me a water jug and told me to drink. I managed to swallow a few mouthfuls, then puked it up. "I gotta lie down."

Tim helped me to the tent. I crawled inside.

"Don't worry, I'm not gonna die," I told him.

"You better not." His face was drawn and pale.

"I'm cold."

He covered me with a blanket.

"I'm just gonna lie here a while." The last light of dusk filtered through the tent fabric. I could hear Tim breathing, and the muted rumbling of the rapids. I closed my eyes and saw a sea of bald heads, I saw Harryette and Emory, I saw Frosty and Tim skidding down the scree, I saw Uncle and Hap in the Land Rover, searching for us. I saw the trail, rocky and steep, infinitely long. Images came and went, like a slide show. The Kinka pissing at Moran Point. Trout flapping at the end of my line. The giant boulder tipping into the canyon. I watched as it crashed though rock and trees, sailing over the Redwall, tumbling across the Tonto Platform, falling into the inner gorge, sending a plume of water a thousand feet high. Warm water rained down upon me.

Something wet, dragging across my face, and voices. I opened my eyes, saw a pale, oval shape hovering over me.

"Why is the water warm?" I asked.

"Drink," said the voice, low and light.

Arms lifted me to a sitting position; a cup found my lips. I gulped.

"Slowly." A girl's voice.

I drank until the cup was empty, then fell back into my dreams.

I drift downstream, water lapping at my sides. The canyon walls rise to the sky, the buttes march slowly past, sluggish monsters made of billion-year-old stone. I roll over rapids, rocks soft as gelatin, float through dark parapets of the Vishnu Schist, rock formed when the earth was a lifeless, molten ball. Ahead, a bridge, a figure standing upon it. The Phantom watches me pass, a smile upon her calm face.

Suddenly I am spinning, caught in a whirlpool, the water falling into a great, dark hole. I begin to swim, frantically grasping handholds in the water, dragging myself up the sides of the whirling funnel. I look back. The hole is growing larger, and now I can see light below. The tops of trees, rolling green hills, a meandering turquoise stream. The sides of the funnel have become almost vertical, as sheer as the Redwall. I kick and claw my way up the wall of water, gasping.

Voices.

The tent was bright with mottled sunlight, my mouth dry as ash. My leg? I felt only a heaviness there. I heard Tim talking, his voice low, then a second, higher voice. Harryette? No, it was the voice from my dreams. I raised my head and looked down my body. My foot was propped up on a rolled blanket, wrapped in a bird's nest of leaves and grass. Only my toes, gray and dead looking, were visible. I willed them to move. The big toe responded, bending lightly, sending prickles of pain up my shin. I sat up, moving carefully, and rolled over onto my hands and knees. The pain was bearable. I lifted the tent flap and looked out. Tim, sitting on a log in front of the dead fire, was talking to a black-haired girl. She heard me moving and found me with eyes dark as obsidian.

"He is back," she said.

ISABELLA

I CRAWLED OUT OF THE TENT; Tim jumped up to help me to my feet. I tried to put weight on my right foot, but almost passed out from the pain.

The girl, her expression placid, said, "You must wait for the poison to leave your body."

Tim helped me sit down. He poured some water into a cup and gave it to me to drink. "You're going to be all right," he said. "The bandage will suck the poison out."

"That's a bandage?" I asked, looking at the crudely tied mass of vegetation wrapping my ankle.

"A poultice," said the girl.

I took a good look at her. She appeared to be about my age. Her skin was golden with sun, her mouth wide, her eyes sleepy. She wore a tattered pair of blue jeans and a long-sleeved shirt with snap buttons and embroidery over each pocket. Her feet were bare. A pair of battered hiking boots sat on the ground beside her. She had a knife on her belt, and her long black hair was tied back with a braided cord.

"Who are you?"

"My name is Isabella." Her lips parted, showing brilliant white teeth.

"What are you doing here?"

"I saw your fire."

"Where did you come from?"

She pointed downriver. I looked to Tim, hoping for a better explanation.

"She helped me take care of you," Tim said. "She showed up just after you passed out. She knows about snakebites and stuff."

"You live down here?" I asked.

"I am alive, and I am here."

"That's not what I meant."

"I am a traveler, like you."

A wave of exhaustion passed through me. I closed my eyes.

"You must sleep again."

"I don't want to sleep."

"You will."

"I had dreams."

"Everyone dreams. This is how we know ourselves."

Fragments of dream memory came and went. Warm water, carrying me through the canyon. The whirlpool. Knowledge bloomed inside me, a terrible hollowness, and dread. My eyes filled with tears. I turned to Tim.

"I know why the water is warm," I said.

He looked at me.

I said, "They never opened the gates. If they'd opened the gates the water would be cold."

"No," said Tim.

"It's coming over the top, Tim. They never got there. The water's warm because it's not coming from the bottom of the lake. It's coming over the top of the dam."

Tim's mouth grew small and tight. He walked out of the grove toward the river, stood and stared down at the rushing rapids. I could see from the set of his shoulders that the news had hit him hard. If Hap and Uncle had not opened the gates, it was a sure thing they hadn't made it to Page. And that probably meant the worst.

Isabella said, "I don't understand. What dam?"

"The Glen Canyon Dam. Only now it's the Glen Canyon *Falls*."

"It must be very beautiful. Why is this a bad thing?"

"Because it means his father—and my uncle . . ." I couldn't finish.

Isabella came to sit before me. She leaned forward, looking into my face. "Your eyes are sad."

She was altogether too calm. I wanted to shake her up, to make her feel some of my despair. I cleared my throat. "We're all gonna be sad pretty soon, when that dam goes."

"And when might that be?"

"Next week. Next year. Who knows?"

She considered that.

"It will not matter," she said at last, standing up in a single, fluid motion. Something about the shape of her body, the way she was standing, made me remember.

"I know who you are," I said.

She smiled. "Who am I?"

"You're the Phantom." I pointed downstream, in the direction of Phantom Ranch. "You found Cecil for me."

She laughed, a joyful chortle from deep inside, and I felt a weird moment of happiness, a sense that everything would be okay. I squeezed my eyes shut and tried to hold on to the sensation, letting the sound of her laughter echo through my thoughts.

I slept again with the sun beating down upon me, and I dreamed. I saw Isabella's face, felt her hands on my cheeks, heard her voice. Then I fell, as if the edge of the world had crumbled, canyon walls rushing toward the sky. Isabella was falling with me, and as we fell she said, with perfect calmness, "It will not matter, Ceej."

And in my dream, I believed her.

The next time I woke up it was late afternoon. Isabella was down at the river fishing for trout with a hand line. Tim sat beside the fire, watching me. I crawled over to sit beside him.

"How are you feeling?" he asked.

"Better. I had some weird dreams. I was falling, and Isabella was falling with me."

He threw another stick on the fire. "You think she's crazy?"

"Maybe we're all crazy."

"She told me she's been walking through the canyon for a month. She knows what plants to eat and stuff. She thinks she's going to meet up with her people. She says she's a Hopi, but she grew up in Las Vegas. Anyway, the Hopi are all dead. They got the Flu early on."

"Did you tell her that?"

"That's what's weird. I think she knows it. She knows they're dead, but she's still planning on joining them. She's a strange one."

I had to agree. "You think she might want to stay with us?"

"You mean here in Hotel Mesquite?"

"I mean when we leave."

"I don't know. She has some place she's trying to get to. Some sort of religious place. She has maps, she says. You know what she calls the canyon? *Awn-toop-ka.* I think she's sick in the head."

"Maybe she'll come with us." My leg was starting to throb again.

Tim shrugged. "How soon do you think you'll be able to walk?"

I tried to imagine walking. Isabella had changed the poultice and I'd seen my ankle, all purple and red and swollen. The thought of it made my leg hurt worse.

"I could ride on Cecil."

Tim looked away. "Cecil's gone."

"Gone?"

"He wandered off yesterday. I spent most of the day looking for him."

"You didn't tie him up?"

He gave me an angry, embarrassed look. "Hey, I had *you* to worry about."

"So it's *my* fault?" It felt good to get mad.

Tim shrugged, his jaw clenched. For a moment I thought we were going to get into a big argument, but then Isabella appeared holding a fat trout in each hand.

"The river has given us a meal," she said, grinning. She looked so happy and proud that all the anger went out of me. I wanted to touch her smile.

Dinner that night was fresh trout, crackers, and some shoots Isabella had gathered downstream in a little backwater. The fish was delicious, but the shoots tasted like mud. I ate my share, even though I didn't have much of an appetite. The pain in my leg and foot had subsided, but I was feeling heavy in my body, as if I had a belly full of sand. After we ate, Isabella changed the poultice again. The swelling in my ankle had subsided. Her hands were gentle and firm.

"You are healing," she said. "You are strong."

"I don't feel strong."

She grasped my biceps and squeezed. "Strong," she said, grinning. In the half light of canyon dusk her skin became darker, her teeth whiter.

Tim, sitting a few yards away, asked her when I would be able to travel.

"That is for Ma'saw to decide," she replied.

"Who?"

"The Guardian. He who permits us to leave our footprints upon this place."

"That's crazy," Tim said. "All that Indian stuff."

I held my breath, surprised that Tim would say such a thing.

Isabella cocked her head, giving him a half frown, half smile. "You are here in Öngtupqa, yet you are blind to all that surrounds you. So typical of a *pahanna*."

"'Awn-toop-ka?' I thought we were in the Grand Canyon."

"Öngtupqa is the Hopi name."

"I wish you'd talk English."

"I wish *you'd* speak Hopi."

"I wish you'd stand on your head and sing marching songs."

Isabella's mouth fell open and she laughed. Her laughter filled the mesquite grove, shaking the leaves, and in a second Tim was laughing, too.

I said, "I think you're both nuts."

Isabella's mouth clamped shut. "That's not very nice," she said. She glared at me for a heartbeat, then she and Tim burst into laughter, again. I glowered at the two of them, feeling left out. I didn't understand how Tim could insult her, then make everything funny and okay again with a few words. He thought Isabella was crazy, but he seemed at ease in her company. They bantered back and forth as easily as people in movies, arguing and joking, enjoying themselves. Later, sitting around the fire, Tim told her the story of how I'd hidden the truck horn under his bed, and we were all laughing together. Then Isabella told us about her grandfather, who had spent four years traveling the canyon on foot.

"My grandfather was of the Crow Clan. He lived in Oraibi, the old village on Third Mesa. When he was a young man he fell in love with a Navajo girl, who rejected him. Broken in his heart, he felt the call of Öngtupqa, the canyon. Wearing moccasins and carrying a pack he sewed himself from the hide of an elk"— she pointed at her battered leather backpack—"he journeyed on foot from Hopi, across the lands controlled by the Navajo to the Salt Trail, where he descended into the gorge. He sought out the *Sipapuni*, the place of emergence, and camped there for four days and four nights. On the fourth night, he spoke with Ma'saw, the guardian of the Fourth World. Ma'saw commanded my grandfather to remain in Öngtupqa until his memories of the Navajo girl were no more than the shadows of birds flitting across his heart.

"For four years he lived here in Öngtupqa, exploring its shadows and learning its ways. One day he awakened to find a mockingbird perched on a branch above him. 'You have healed yourself,' said the mockingbird. 'It is time for you to leave this place and rejoin your people.'

"My grandfather looked into his heart and found that the darkness there had lifted, and when he thought of his Navajo love, he felt only wisps of sadness.

"Returning to Hopi, he told his stories to the men in the kiva, and he became an important man. Very soon after his return, he married a Hopi girl—my grandmother. My father was born the following year in Oraibi.

"My father grew quickly. Like a weed, Grandfather said. Years passed like leaves blowing in the wind. When my father was old enough to work, he left Walpi for Flagstaff, where he found a job as a carpenter, and where he met my mother. They married and moved to Las Vegas. My father became a security guard at a casino."

"Was your mother Hopi?" Tim asked.

"Actually, she was Italian."

"You're only half Hopi, then."

"No. I am all Hopi."

"But you never lived on the reservation."

"I would visit my grandfather at Oraibi. Later, when he was very old, my grandfather came to live with us in Las Vegas. My parents told me it was because he could not take care of himself, but the real reason he came was to teach me. He told me the ways of my people, how we emerged into this world, and our place in it."

I asked, "What was that word you used before— seepa pooni?"

Isabella said, "I will tell you the story of my people. *Haliksa'i!*"

"Bless you," said Tim.

Isabella frowned. "*Haliksa'i* means listen."

"Okay, okay."

"Many years ago, long before the grandfathers of our grandfather's great grandfathers were born, people lived in the Third World, a land of rolling, grassy hills, clear waters, and gentle sun. They had lived there for many generations, and they were happy, but life was too easy. In time, the people became lazy. Many of the priests and the witches turned to evil, and their wickedness tainted the people around them. Men began to steal from one another. Instead of tending their crops, they spent their time gambling in the kivas, and the women joined them. Corn wilted in the fields. Children cried for food.

"Those who remained virtuous tried to change things, but they were ignored, so they decided to seek a better place. They sent a catbird high into the sky to search for new lands. When the catbird returned, he told how he had passed through a sipapu in the sky and there discovered a vast new land."

"Isn't 'sipapu' the thing you said your grandpa camped by?" Tim asked.

"A *sipapu* is a hole. *Haliksa'i!* So the virtuous people, after some discussion, decided to journey to the Upper World. They planted a bamboo stalk, and they prayed and chanted, and the stalk grew up through the clouds. The people gathered up all their pots and tools and clothing and food and began to climb, but the way was long, and as they climbed they had to lighten their load. By the time they reached the sipapu in the sky they had cast away all their possessions."

"They were naked?"

Isabella gave him a frowning look. "I don't know. Maybe they still had clothes. It's not important. They emerged from the Sipapuni and found themselves here, in Öngtupqa. And that is why we call this the Fourth World."

"What about the First and Second Worlds?"

"Those worlds are lost to memory."

"What's the Sipapuni? Is it the same as *sipapu?*"

"The Sipapuni is the place of emergence. There is only one Sipapuni. There are many sipapus. From the Third World, the Sipapuni is a sipapu in the sky. Here, it is a sipapu in the earth."

"A hole?"

Isabella nodded and pointed upriver. "It is where my grandfather met Ma'saw. It is where I am going."

Tim turned to me. "I told you she was nuts."

One of the more remarkable results of the multiple decimations caused by the Flu has been the revival of ancient belief systems. Highly organized religions such as the Islam, Catholic, and Protestant faiths, all of which relied heavily on their bureaucracies, have disappeared in many regions of North America, while many of the more obscure religions—Wicca, Christian Science, and several African and Native American belief systems—have flourished.

Some religious leaders have decried this shift in faiths as a return to the primitive—but the more common explanation is that the Flu simply leveled the playing field. With the collapse of their infrastructure, the big religions lost their competitive edge.

—from A Recent History of the Human Race by P. D. Boggs ©2038

PART TWO:

BELLA

TO THE RIM

Granddaughter?
Yes, Grandfather?
You have come far.
Yes, Grandfather.
You are very close now.
Yes, Grandfather.
But you have far to travel.
Not too far, I hope.
Your journey continues.
Alone?
Not alone. You are never alone.

THE DARK-HAIRED BOY, CEEJ, is for me. His arms are long and his hands are large, but he carries his heaviness in his heart. He needs me to guide him through this place of death and life. It is for him I have been waiting, for it would be a sad thing to leave this world alone.

The other, the small one called Tim, has feet that remain always on the soil of this world. He does not trust me, but the other needs him. We are together here.

• • •

I lay out my possessions on a flat white stone. I have a small aluminum cooking pot and a butane lighter, the last of three. I have my grandfather's notebook showing the secret ways in and out of Öngtupqa. I have a small cloth bag filled with dried berries, another filled with mesquite beans, and a smaller one filled with crumbly yellow earth. I have the kachina doll my grandfather made for me when I was a little girl. She is called *Palhikwmana,* or Moisture Maiden. She is small and crudely carved from the root of a cottonwood tree. Her headdress is broken down to ragged nubbins and one arm has broken off. Today she looks angry. I wrap her in soft cloth.

I have a $5 poker chip from the casino where my father worked. I have my red and black Polarfleece blanket and an extra pair of socks and an old woolen sweater and a sheet of plastic big enough to hide under when it rains. I have my knife and my coil of nylon rope and two plastic water bottles and a river stone that looks like the head of a tortoise and everything fits inside my elkhide backpack. These are my possessions.

I feel wealthy.

In the morning, Ceej is able to walk, though with great pain. I tell him to wait, to rest yet another day, but he forces his swollen foot into his boot. He has a sister, he says, who needs his help. I understand this.

His family holds him here. His sister calls to him, and her power is the greater. Tim also feels this call, and I see that she is a part of him, too. They tell me of the Kinka. I have heard of these Kinka, who believe that this world has become their own. Perhaps they are right.

I spend the afternoon searching for the mule, Cecil. His tracks take me upriver, and then disappear among the rocks, and I realize that this time the mule does not wish to be found. I return to the camp by the rapids, where the boys are waiting. I tell them that the mule has chosen his own path. Tim rolls his eyes, but Ceej nods. He understands.

I show them my grandfather's notebook, the maps he made sixty years ago. It shows forty-seven trails in and out of Öngtupqa, many of them secret and known only to my people. The boys pore over the maps, asking me questions. I point out the fastest route to the rim, but they do not want to go that way. It is the way they came in. They fear the Kinka. I show them another trail, a longer way.

"That must be the Grandview Trail," Ceej says.

I do not know the names he uses. In Grandfather's notebook it is called the High Spring Trail. By either name, I tell them, it will take two days, perhaps longer, because of Ceej's foot. Still, they wish to go on, and I see that it is their destiny to do so.

But what of my destiny? One, perhaps two days of following the river will bring me to the Sipapuni. I do not wish to turn aside when I am so close, but it is clear to me that my path now lies with these two white boys. I gather up Grand-father's elkhide pack and prepare to join them.

"You don't have to come with us," Tim says.

"You are wrong," I tell him.

In the morning I brew a stimulating tonic from the hard green stems of the pale green shrub known as Mormon Tea. It is called this because it was drunk by the Mormons when they first encountered Öngtupqa a century before my grandfather was born. The boys make faces at its bitterness, and Tim refuses to drink all of his, but I am happy when Ceej swallows the last drop. It will energize him for the journey ahead.

The first day takes us back along the trail I have been following, up onto the plateau that divides the inner gorge from the upper canyon. The Tonto Platform, Ceej calls it. He must stop to rest often. I can see that he is in pain. As we walk, he asks me questions about my life before the plague. It seems a thousand years ago, living in Las Vegas with my parents and my grandfather, going to school with hundreds of other children, watching television.

I did not care about being Hopi back then. I wished only to be accepted by the other children, to have fun, to play little girl games. The tales my grandfather told me seemed like fables, stories told by an old man to entertain his granddaughter. Ma'saw, God of the Fourth World, was no more real to me than Santa Claus or the Tooth Fairy.

My occasional visits to Hopi were holidays, a chance to miss some school and play with my cousins—three boys, younger than me, all filled with life and joy and mischief. The symbols on the Hopi jewelry and pottery meant nothing to me. The thousand-year-old homes in Oraibi seemed like play houses. When the men descended into their kivas to smoke and chant, and my cousins went off to play their little boy games, my great aunt and I would make *piki,* that crumbly blue bread made of blue corn, ash and fat, rolled into sheets so thin you can see through it. It was all great fun, but no more important or true than Disneyland, or the casinos of Las Vegas. Or so I believed.

Then the Flu came to Las Vegas and took my parents. I fled the city with my grandfather. For seven years we lived in a cabin in the Virgin Mountains near Lake Mead where he taught me the ways of the Hopi. He taught me how to survive in a world destroyed. He taught me the secrets of the kiva, things that only the men were supposed to know. He told me that one day, when I was older, he would take me to the Sipapuni, and that we would rejoin our people there.

And then one morning I tried to wake him, but he was cold. He had died and left me, like all the rest of them. Grandfather was the only person I ever knew who died from something besides the Flu.

As we near the great limestone cliff called the Redwall, Ceej suddenly collapses, unconscious. I think that the pain has been worse than we knew. Tim and I make him as comfortable as we can, and I unwrap his poultice, expecting the worst.

The foot is ugly, but there is no infection, and when I pinch his little toe he groans and pulls his foot away.

"He will be fine," I tell Tim.

"What do you mean? Look at him!" Tim is angry. In that moment, he thinks that he is mad at me. I accept his anger without striking back. He has to put it someplace.

Ceej comes around in a few minutes and demands to know what happened.

"You passed out," Tim tells him.

Ceej tries to stand up, but I won't let him.

"You must let me wrap your ankle," I say. "And we must rest a while."

Ceej is furious and embarrassed, but he lets me minister to him. I make a fresh poultice using redbud leaves, and a paste of pounded juniper berries and yellow earth. My small pouch of the powdered yellow-orange clay is almost gone.

"What is that stuff?" Ceej asks.

"It is a special clay gathered by my grandfather at

the Sipapuni. It will help draw the poison from your wound." I wrap the poultice with fibrous strips from a nearby yucca plant. "Grandfather used it for bee stings. It has great power."

Tim makes a snorting sound. He shoulders his pack. "I'm gonna take a look up ahead," he says, and moves up the trail.

I stretch Ceej's sock back over his foot to hold the poultice together. When I look up, he is staring at me. His eyes are the color of mesquite heartwood: a brown that is almost black, but with a hint of fire.

"Thank you," he says.

I look away. I am embarrassed, but I do not know why. I feel his hand touch my knee. I don't move; I don't breathe.

He says, "What did your parents call you?"

"My name is Isabella."

"I mean at home. Like, my real name is Charles Jacob Kane, but everybody calls me Ceej. For C. J. Did your folks call you Isabella?"

"My mother did." I feel something inside crumbling. "But Daddy called me Bella."

I see Ceej's hand coming to my face, and he touches the corner of my eyes, and his fingers are wet with tears.

"Bella," he says, touching my tears to his cheek. Our eyes meet and the crumbling inside me becomes something else. I want to fall into him, but I turn away, suddenly afraid, and we sit in silence.

A few minutes later, Tim returns.

"There's a spring up ahead," he says. "Fresh water."

The spring is a small, algae-lined pool tucked into the base of the Redwall. The area is shaded by junipers, and a single tamarisk looking uneasy and alone so high up in the canyon. I make a thin porridge of cornmeal, sugar, and water, and we all drink a cup for strength. As my body takes in the sugar and corn, my eyes open to the perfect beauty of this place. Grandfather, as a young man, rested in this same shady spot, perhaps drinking a fortifying cornmeal gruel. The river below forms a turquoise vein. I think about what Tim and Ceej have told me about the dam. If it should fail, the flood would destroy much. But as Grandfather often said, "What will happen will happen, and it will be right." For years, I resisted this truth, but my months in Öngtupqa have shown me that Grandfather was correct. Somehow, although I do not understand how or why, even the Flu must be right—terribly right.

Ceej insists that he can continue, and so we do. As we trudge slowly upward, Tim in the lead, I tell Ceej the story of how Mockingbird gave the tribes different languages.

"After the people emerged from the Sipapuni, there remained many disagreements, for even good people have differences. The chiefs and the medicine men called upon Spider Grandmother, who saw that the people were unhappy with themselves.

"'You must leave this place,' she said. 'Each tribe must have its own food, its own language, its own land.'

"'But how can we do this?' asked the chiefs.

"Just then, Mockingbird, who had been listening, brought several ears of corn and laid them upon the earth. One ear was the color of flint, one was the red of these cliffs, one was bright yellow, and one was deep blue, like the sky in the instant before the stars appear in the night. Some ears were speckled, some were long, some were short. 'We begin with the selection of the corn,' said Mockingbird. 'Each color will bring its own future, its own rewards, its own price.'

"The Navajo leader quickly grasped the bright yellow ear. 'You have chosen happiness and prosperity,' Mockingbird told him, 'but the lives of your people will be short.'

"The Utes chose the flint corn, the Comanches the red, and so on. Mockingbird told each of them the paths they had chosen. Finally there was only one left— a small, stubby, misshapen ear of blue that all the other tribes had ignored. The Hopi chief, who had not yet chosen, stepped forward and claimed it. Mockingbird said, 'You have chosen the hardest path, and the longest. Your people will struggle and endure many hardships, but you shall outlive all the rest.'

"And so the Hopi became the people of the short blue corn.

"The next morning, the people awakened and discovered that their mouths and ears had changed. They could talk, but only the people of their own tribe could understand them. They could hear, but could only understand the words of their own tribe. There was great confusion, and the people gathered around the Sipapuni and called for Mockingbird, who could speak many languages.

"Mockingbird settled upon the rim of the Sipapuni and began to speak, and his words were understood by all. 'Now you each have your own corn and your own language. It is time for you to spread out upon this new land. You, the Apache, must travel south to a place beyond the mountains. The Comanche must seek the rising sun. The Navajo must follow the river until the river is no more.' Mockingbird sent each of the tribes in a different direction, until only the Hopi remained. 'You who have chosen the path of hardship face the longest journey. You will build again and again, and each time you will plant your blue corn and you will leave your marks upon the rocks and the earth, and you will travel yet again, and one day you will find your homeland in a place not far from here. Your home will be a land of harsh beauty, and it will be preserved for you.'"

I am not sure Ceej is listening. His footsteps have grown shorter and less certain, and I fear he is going to fall down again. But then he says, "Why did the Hopi wait to choose?"

"According to my grandfather, it was because they

knew their destiny from the beginning. 'What happened was what must have happened,' he liked to say."

For a time, we walk without speaking, listening only to the sound of wind on stone.

We camp above the Redwall, beneath a rogue ponderosa pine. The rim is less than a thousand feet above us. We do not make a fire because the boys are afraid that it might be seen by the Kinka. The moon has yet to rise, and it is very dark. Ceej asks me to tell him more about the Sipapuni. He wants to know if it is a real place or just an idea.

"My grandfather was there," I tell him. "It is real."

Tim says, "Yeah, like the Fountain of Youth."

"That may also be real," I say. "You do not know."

He makes a sputtering sound with his lips and turns away.

Ceej says, "What is it, like a big hole in the ground?"

"No. The Sipapuni looks like a beautiful rock, as big as a house, and it contains all the colors of the world. It rests beside the Little Colorado River, one day's walk from where the Little Colorado meets the Colorado."

"I don't get it. I thought you said it was some kind of hole."

"At the top of the Sipapuni is a hole, a sipapu, the point of emergence. My grandfather looked within."

"What did he see?"

"Boiling water, cold to the touch. He believed that when the last of the people emerged from the sipapu they covered it with water so that anyone looking inside would see only a spring."

Ceej thought about that for a moment, then asked, "How do you know it's really real, and not just a story?"

"After Grandfather looked into the Sipapuni, he camped beside it for four days and four nights. At the end of the fourth night, as the sky brightened and the birds began to fill the air with song, he climbed again to the top of the Sipapuni. He lowered his hand into the cold, boiling water. He felt wetness. He pushed his arm deeper and suddenly felt the heat of the sun on his hand. Frightened, he jerked his hand free and for a moment, where his arm had been, there was a hole in the water. He saw another gorge, a river, grasses, trees, and the shadows of clouds."

"It could still be a story."

I shake my head. Even Ceej, who wants so to believe, shares some of Tim's doubts.

"You would not say that if you knew Grandfather." I hold out my arm and, with my finger, draw a circle around it, just below my elbow. "Here, where his arm passed through the sipapu, he had a scar as white as old bone."

Granddaughter?
Yes, Grandfather?

You have told my story well.
Thank you, Grandfather.
You must continue your journey.
I am trying, Grandfather.

The next morning Ceej's foot is much better. After a light breakfast of crackers and dried apples, we head up the final, steep climb. The trail switchbacks up through a forest of pinyon, juniper, and an occasional ponderosa pine. I pick some Mormon Tea growing beside the trail and tell Ceej to chew the stems. Maybe the stimulant in the plant will help him, or maybe just the idea of it will help him. Either way, though his foot is hurting, he keeps up a steady pace.

It takes us less than two hours to reach the rim.

THE RANGER OFFICE

WE ARE WATCHING CHILDREN PLAY. I am sure that the game the three little boys are playing has no name—the rules change from minute to minute. Two of the boys look like twins, blond and blue-eyed. The other boy is darker, his head a mass of shiny curls. Sometimes it looks like they are playing tag, but mostly they are just wrestling and laughing and kicking around a hard white ball.

A yellow bus is parked in the circular driveway in front of the porch. It is as though the children are about to leave for school. They will climb aboard the bus and go to kindergarten. I allow myself to remember what that was like. Sixty chattering, laughing, shrieking kids on the big yellow bus.

But here there are only three children. They are playing the way my cousins used to play, happy and fearless, screaming with excitement as they tumble over each other in the tall grass. Yes, I think they are very much like my cousins—except that these boys are alive, and the ball they are playing with is a human skull.

I am lost here, above the rim, in a world I thought I would never see again.

The childrens' playground is the overgrown front lawn of the El Tovar Hotel, an enormous three-story building made of timbers and stone. Ceej and I are on our bellies in the brush, watching.

The children are not alone. Two adult Kinkas sit on the front porch of the hotel. One is reading a book, the other is sucking her thumb. There are more inside the hotel.

Tim has circled around the other side of the stone building they call the Hopi House. It is not a real Hopi house. Ceej says it's a place where they used to sell T-shirts and kachina dolls to tourists. We can see Tim. He moves his hands, and Ceej signals back. I have never seen them doing this hand-talking before, although Ceej has told me about it.

Ceej whispers to me, "He says there are four more on the rim side, and he can see some moving around inside the hotel." He grabs my arm and points. Two Kinka are coming around the corner of the hotel. One is a young woman wearing blue jeans and a checkered shirt. The other is a dark-skinned woman in a kind of long, glittery golden dress. She has dozens of loops of gold on her wrists and around her neck, and orange lightning bolts painted on her cheeks. The children stop playing as the two women pass through their game. Ceej's fingers are digging into my forearm. The dark woman is talking, gesturing with bangled arms. The other woman watches her, expressionless. There is something about her face. I think for a moment that I know her, but then I see her eyes and I know what it is.

She looks like Ceej.

The women climb the stone steps and enter the hotel. The children resume their play. One of the twins gives the skull a hard kick. It shatters. They are sad for a moment—another broken toy—then they laugh and are playing again, hair flying in the wind. I wonder why these children—these Kinka—are not bald. The weight of the sky presses down upon me, too close, and I know that I am seeing the future.

"I saw her again," Tim says. "She was in one of the third story windows, looking out."

"Did she see you?"

"I don't think so. I saw Emory, too, walking along the rim. He's got his head all painted up. His nose is blue and he's got a yellow lightning bolt on his forehead. And that black woman walking with Harryette? That's the one they call Mother K."

Ceej asks, "Any sign of Hap or Uncle?"

Tim shakes his head.

"We have to figure out a way to talk to Harryette."

"And a way to get her away."

"If she wants to go. She didn't exactly look like a prisoner."

We have retreated to the Ranger Office, across the railroad tracks from El Tovar. The first floor is divided into several rooms: a front office area, a conference room, several small offices and two bathrooms. There is no running water, of course, but we found a full water cooler jug in one of the closets.

Ceej said there used to be some guns stored upstairs. He and Tim went up and looked around, but all they found were about a thousand squeaking bats. They've taken over the whole second floor, and now we know what that weird smell is. It's bat dung.

We have only Ceej's rifle. It doesn't matter. With only three of us against so many Kinka, if it comes to shooting guns it will not matter if we have one gun, or a hundred.

We are in the conference room sitting around a huge table. Ceej and Tim are talking back and forth about buildings I don't know, about guns and alarms and ways to get from one place to another, unseen. I listen to them, understanding little. This is their world; I am a stranger here. I long for Öngtupqa's embrace. Their words blur and become distant. Eventually they wind down as daylight begins to fade. Both boys look older in the half-light. Ceej's face is slack with fatigue.

"You should lie down," I tell him. "There's a sofa in the next room."

Ceej doesn't argue. He stands and limps out of the conference room down the hallway. I use the last gray minutes of dusk to examine his foot and ankle. Nearly all of the swelling is gone, and he says it feels better. The long march from the river to the rim has worked out the last of the poison, and all that is left is for his body to repair the damaged tissues. I make the healing paste of juniper berries and a scant handful of yellow earth. Only a tiny amount remains. Grandfather made his pouch of powdered clay last for fifty years, and I am using the last fine grains to heal this *pahanna*.

The yellow earth is both boon and burden. It has the power to heal, but the clay does not like to be so far from the Sipapuni. One day, Grandfather once told me, he would return the last yellow grains to their source. I hope to carry out his wish.

In the dark, we make a sorry meal of crackers and canned peaches. To pass the time, I ask Ceej to teach me his sign language. Our hands meet in the blackness, and he guides my fingers into the proper shapes. I learn *yes* and *no* and *come* and *go*. He teaches me to sign his name, and Tim's name. He says I can make up my own sign for myself. I come up with a two-handed sign, cupping my hands together. It feels right, but Ceej laughs and tells me I have made the sign for hamburger. He shows me how to finger spell out my name, making a separate sign for each letter. I practice it a few times.

"Where did all the signs come from?" I ask.

"My sister learned most of them from a book, and we made a lot of them up ourselves. Like this——" He makes a V with his hands, pressing the heels of his palms together, his fingers splayed out. "That means Grand Canyon."

"Öngtupqa."

"Yeah. And here's one we made up for the Flu." He

takes my left hand and draws my finger across my throat like he is cutting it.

My lesson continues, but Tim, who has been sitting quietly listening to us, grows restless. Ceej is showing me how to sign *Help, I'm being eaten by wolves,* when Tim announces that it is dark enough. He is going out.

"Wait," says Ceej. "I'll come with you."

"Forget it," Tim says. "You'll just slow me down."

I feel that Ceej is hurt by this. Tim did not have to say it that way, even though it is true. Ceej's leg is much better, but he still moves slowly.

"You should rest tonight," I tell him. "Tomorrow you may need all your strength."

Tim goes out alone.

It is very dark inside the Ranger Office. The moon has not yet risen, and only starlight touches the windows. I can see Ceej's shape, black on black, sitting at the other end of the sofa. I hear mice scurrying along the baseboards, and the squeaking of bats from upstairs.

"Do you ever feel like it's the end of the world?" Ceej asks.

"I thought so until today," I say.

"You don't think so now?"

"Not after seeing those kids."

"Playing with a skull."

"They were born into a world filled with skulls. Did you notice their hair?"

"I noticed that they *had* hair."

"That's why I think it is not the end of the world. Or at least not of *their* world. The Kinka's children are normal. And I do not think that they need to worry about the Flu."

"You think they're immune?"

I nod, but he cannot see me in the dark. "They have inherited immunity from their Kinka parents. It is *their* world now. The children of Survivors will inherit this world."

I hear Ceej breathing. Four feet of black air separates us, but I feel his heartbeat, the beating of a distant drum.

"What about us?" he asks.

"For us, there is another world." My knee touches his. "Show me the sign for love," I say.

"It's too dark. I can't see you."

I reach out. "Show me with your hands."

Slowly, he takes my hands in his and closes them into fists. He crosses my wrists and presses my fists into my chest, one fist over each breast. "There." His breath is sweet with the smell of canned peaches. I feel his arms surround me. He whispers something in my ear.

"What's that?" I ask, my voice hoarse.

"Not the end," he says again. Our lips touch.

Granddaughter?
Yes, Grandfather?
You are not alone.

I open my eyes to the gray light of early dawn. My hair is hanging across my face. I brush it aside with my left hand and see Tim, sitting in a chair, staring at me with a peculiar expression on his face. I try to sit up, but something heavy holds me down. Ceej's arm. We are tangled together on the sofa beneath an old blanket. I nudge Ceej. He mutters something, raises his head, blinks. I squirm out from his embrace. My bare feet hit the floor. I stand, pulling the blanket with me, wrapping it around me.

Ceej says, "Hey!" I pick up my clothing and walk into the next room and close the door.

As I dress I can hear their low voices. I move closer to the door.

Tim: "She has to come with us. I know she will."

Ceej: "What if she doesn't want to?"

"She has to. The Kinka are insane. They're like animals."

At first I think they are talking about me, but then I hear Ceej say, "Yeah, but she's one of them. She's a Survivor." I realize they are talking about the sister. I don't know if I'm disappointed or relieved. I tie my hair back with a leather cord, then rejoin them. Ceej is still on the sofa. He is wearing his jeans, but no shirt. Tim is chewing on a strip of jerky. They are talking intently. Neither of them look at me.

Tim says, "They've got the Jeep, the Land Rover, and the bus. That's it. All we have to do is disable the Land Rover. Pull the plug wires loose or something. Then we take off in the Jeep. There's no way they'll catch us, not with just that big bus."

"How do we get Harryette to the Jeep?"

"I'll go in and get her."

"You'll just stroll in and ask her to come with you?"

"Something like that." Tim has been out all night. His eyes are bright, but bruised-looking. I sit down beside Ceej on the sofa.

"You should rest," I tell Tim. He ignores me.

"Tonight, as soon as it gets dark, you pull the wires on the Land Rover, and I'll get Harryette."

"How will you know where she is?" I ask.

This time he looks at me, his face dead with fatigue. "She's in El Tovar. I know which room."

"You saw her?"

"I talked to her."

This takes both Ceej and me by surprise.

Tim says, "She was standing in one of the third-story windows, looking out. I found a place where she could see me. She was surprised."

"What did you tell her?" Ceej asks.

"What d'you think? I told her we were gonna get her out of there." Tim turns his head away from us and rubs his eyes.

"What did she say?" I ask.

Ignoring me, he says, "I watched the Kinka all night long. They spent most of the night in the lobby, sitting around the fireplace like we used to, talking. Some time around midnight they all went to different rooms and went to sleep. That's when I'll get her. There are lots of ways to get into the hotel. I'll get her out of there."

Ceej says, "Why didn't you just tell her to meet us at the Jeep?"

"I have to go get her myself."

"Why?"

Tim shrugs. "She told me to go away."

"Did you ask her about Hap and Uncle?"

"Yeah." His face seems to collapse. "She said they're dead." He draws a shuddering breath. "She said we'll be dead, too, if we don't get out of here."

I listen to Ceej and Tim talking, arguing, scheming. They will not leave without Harryette, this much is clear. Tim believes he can talk her into coming with us. Ceej is not so sure, but he feels they must try.

They are planning so that they will not have to think. The news of their elders' deaths has hit them hard, but as long as they stay focused on Harryette they won't have time to grieve. When night comes again, they decide, they will act. Eventually, their talk grinds down. Tim hasn't slept since the night before last, on the trail. He stretches out on the floor, head cradled in the crook of his elbow, and falls asleep. I look at Ceej. He is staring at the floor. I am feeling shy, too.

He says, "I dreamed that we were all Kinkas."

I reach over and touch my finger to his lips. They tighten. I stand up, walk around behind him, put my hands on his shoulders and begin to massage the muscles on either side of his neck. They are like stone, hard with fear and doubt.

"Don't think," I whisper. "Lie down."

Slowly, I knead away the tightness. My hands are made for this body. I feel his breathing grow deep and slow, and within minutes he is asleep. I continue to massage, gently, until all traces of tension are gone and his face is young again, then I lay down beside him and close my eyes.

> *Granddaughter?*
> *Yes, Grandfather?*
> *You must continue your journey.*
> *Not without the boy.*
> *Then you must bring the boy.*
> *The boy will not come without the sister.*
> *Then you must bring the sister.*
> *I know that.*
> *You must continue your journey.*
> *I know that.*
> *There is a way.*

I open my eyes and quietly sit up. Ceej and Tim are both sleeping soundly. I tiptoe out of the room and down the hall into the next office. I find what I need in one of the desk drawers—a disposable razor.

Another drawer produces scissors. I wipe the dust from a mirror hanging on the wall and take a good look at myself. I am like a wild woman, my hair thick and tangled, my face hardened by months of living in Öngtupqa.

I begin the cutting.

MOTHER K

THE FIRST KINKA I ENCOUNTER is a girl, no older than me, her belly full of child. She is sitting alone on the stone wall in front of Hopi House staring at nothing, or perhaps staring into her own soul. I say hello, but she does not respond.

"Are you all right?" I ask.

She smiles and places her hands on her belly, but will not meet my eyes.

I am standing in the full light of the midday sun. I can feel the heat of it on my skull. I turn toward the hotel. Several Kinka are lounging on the porch, talking. I climb the stone steps. There are four of them, three men and one woman. All of them have paint on their skulls and faces. They stop talking as I walk past them and push through the door to the hotel lobby, feeling naked.

Inside, a small fire is burning in a huge stone fireplace, but the lobby is empty. Dead animal heads hang from the walls. Tim saw Harryette on the third floor. I start up the stairway leading to the mezzanine. I hear the lobby door open behind me, but I do not look back. In one of the long hallways leading from the mezzanine I see a boy in his late teens. He is feeling his way along the wall, counting out loud as he reaches each doorway. Sensing me, he stops.

"Is this the second floor?" he asks.

"Yes," I tell him.

His brow contorts. "I have not heard you before."

"I'm new."

"Are you . . . ?" He moves closer and reaches for me, his hand high. He wants to touch my head, so I bow slightly and step into his hand. His fingers dance lightly over my scalp and he says, "Ahhh. You are Kinka."

"Yes." At least I've fooled one of them.

"My name is Alan," he says.

"I'm Isabella."

"I'm blind. Are you blind?"

"No."

"That's good." He nods, a habit left over from the days when he could see.

"I heard there was another new girl," I say. "Do you know where she is?"

"Her name is Harryette," the boy says, smiling. "But she can't talk." His smile fades. A girl who cannot speak is of little use to a blind boy.

"Where is she?"

"She is with Mother K."

"Who is Mother K?" I ask.

A deep voice comes from behind me.

"*I* am Mother K."

I turn. She is tall and thin, her body covered by a long lavender robe, her arms caught in a swirl of golden rings, the black pupils of her eyes surrounded by disks of amber, slashes of orange paint zigzagging across her cheeks. Her skin is darker than mine. Her lips are full and her nose is broad. She is the most beautiful and frightening woman I have ever seen.

Standing behind her is Ceej's sister, Harryette.

Mother K's golden eyes burn into me. She says, "We do not know you, child."

I do not know what else to do, so I offer her my hand. "My name is Isabella."

She does not look at my hand.

"Come with Mother K," she says. She whirls and heads back toward the mezzanine. Her robe touches the floor so that her feet are not visible. She seems to glide along the carpeted hallway. Harryette falls in behind us. I want to sign to her, but I am afraid it will be seen. We go down the staircase to the lobby. Someone has added a broken wooden chair to the fire, and it is blazing. Mother K leads me to the sofa nearest the hearth. We sit down. Harryette stands behind the sofa. Several other Kinka have entered the lobby and are looking at me curiously. I can feel the heat of the fire on my right side. Mother K places her hand atop my head and fixes her amber eyes on a place somewhere inside my skull. I return her gaze, trying not to tremble as her eyes bore holes into my soul.

"Isabella," she says, smiling. Her teeth are large, white, and regular. "So, you have come to join us?"

"Yes."

"And from where have you come, child?"

"I don't know."

Mother K's eyebrows arch in disbelief.

"I have been traveling for a long time," I say.

"Alone? With nothing?"

"I need little."

Harryette has moved to the end of the sofa where I can see her.

Mother K turns to the group of Kinka standing behind us. "She comes from nowhere with nothing!"

The Kinka laugh. Harryette's eyes are upon me. I cup my right hand into a C, then make a J with my little finger——Ceej's name. Harryette's eyes widen.

Mother K says, "And why do you wish to join us?"

"There are stories . . . people talk of you . . . the Kinka. You are powerful."

"And how is that?"

The fire is hot on my right leg, on my cheek.

"You bring death."

Mother K throws her head back and laughs. "Death? You are misinformed, child."

"You bring the Flu." Looking past Mother K, I see Harryette signing to me, but her hands are moving too fast, and I don't know the signs she is using.

"That is true," says Mother K. She places her palms together, and I see the rest of the Kinka repeat her gesture. There are more of them now. They have been coming in by ones and twos. "The Flu is a test, a transformation, an opportunity to become more than what we were. For some it is a release from this world. Either way, we bring the future. You have seen our children?" Mother K smiles proudly.

"Yes."

"The Flu is nothing to them. Not even a sneeze."

"But you kill. The Flu kills."

"Not all. It did not kill me, nor any of my people." She gestures with her long fingers and I see that there are several dozen Kinka watching us. I see the three little boys staring at me wide eyed.

Mother K brings her face close to mine. "What about you? You are a Survivor?" Her breath smells like flowers left too long in a vase.

I nod, forcing myself to stare into her eyes.

"You are a very curious Survivor," she says. Her long hand touches my scalp, stroking. She smiles, her mouth inches from my eyes. Stroking me from my forehead to the nape of my neck. Then she reverses direction, pulling her hand over my scalp from back to front. I feel her palm dragging across invisible bristle.

"Most of us need not shave our heads," she says.

I feel hands on my arms, clamping down hard. Mother K sits back and smiles. Her teeth are plentiful and large and white.

"Let us show her the future," she says.

Hands lift and pull me toward the lobby door.

Grandfather?

I am being walked down the driveway, a Kinka on either side. I try to break free, but their hands are on me like iron manacles.

"Where are you taking me?"

They do not reply. I look back and see Mother K walking a few paces behind us. Harryette is beside her, gesturing urgently, but Mother K will not look at her. The rest of the Kinka are following them in a loose, chattering, excited crowd. They walk me down the short, steep hill, then around to the back of the hotel. There is a separate building there, a windowless structure tucked into the shadow of El Tovar. The door is held shut with a heavy chain secured by a carriage bolt. I realize that the chain is not to keep people out. It is to keep something in. One of the Kinka holds me while the other unscrews the bolt that holds the chain together.

Mother K comes close to me. Her hands grasp my face firmly but gently. She plants a kiss on my forehead.

"Do not be afraid," she says in my ear. "Some do not die."

The door swings open.

I hear coughing.

DEAD MEN

THE DOOR SLAMS SHUT BEHIND ME. The room reeks of rust and rot and grease and urine and sweat and worse. I stand with my back to the door, waiting for my eyes to adjust to the darkness. Light seeps in through vents and cracks in the walls. I see a looming shape, a giant metal monster sprouting pipes and wires.

A man's voice says, "Who are you?"

I look toward the sound and see a pile of rags on the floor against the far wall. My eyes adjust further and the pile of rags becomes a man hugging his knees to his chest. He coughs, a dry cough that starts high in his throat, then works its way down until it becomes a bubbling chortle.

"Who are *you?*" I ask after his hacking subsides.

"You don't know?" The voice is weaker.

"No. They just put me in here. What is this place?"

More coughing; I can feel it echoing in my chest.

"Boiler room. You aren't one of 'em?"

"No."

Silence. "You just natural bald?"

"I shaved my head."

"You're a girl, aren't you?"

I hear a moan, and see the second man lying on his back a few feet away.

"Is he okay?" I ask.

"No. Look, if you're not one of 'em, you better stay away from us."

"You have the Flu."

"That's right, kid." He starts coughing again and tucks his face into his shoulder to muffle it. I am breathing shallowly through my nose. I move a few steps away and run into a spider web. Something scurries across my shaven head; I swat at it and feel my hand wrapped in fine, sticky webbing. I move back toward the door, hoping I have not disturbed a black widow.

The man's coughing fit passes. He clears his throat and says, "They'll leave you in here with us till you get good and sick. That's how they do it. They infect one at a time. They put him"—he gestured toward the unconscious man—"in with poor Sandy a week ago. Then when he got to coughing, they put me in here to keep him company." He laughed, but not in a happy way. "Keeping the virus alive."

"Who's Sandy?"

"Girl they picked up in Page. She's dead now. Just like he's gonna be pretty soon. Like we're all gonna be. This is how these crazies spread the Flu. They always keep a few sick people with 'em. You're next in line, I guess. Sorry, kid."

"Are you Hap, or Uncle?"

Several seconds of silence. "I'm Hap Gordon. He's Chandler Kane. How do you know who we are?"

"Ceej and Tim told me all about you."

"They're . . .?"

"They're here, hiding in the Ranger Office."

"Those damn fool kids," he says, his voice suddenly stronger. "You tell them—aw, hell, you can't tell them anything, can you."

I pull on the door handle and hear the clank of the chain links tightening.

"I don't think so," I say.

> *Grandfather?*
> *Yes, child.*
> *I may never reach the Sipapuni.*
> *What is right is right.*
> *Grandfather?*

Hours pass. I sit with my back against the door, breathing tainted air. The slivers of light from the vents turn gray, then fold into blackness as night surrounds the building. Hap Gordon has slipped into a fitful sleep. I listen to his ragged, liquid breathing. The other man, Ceej's uncle, lies still and silent. I think he must be dead. I stare into the darkness and see motes of light, millions of them, smaller than the smallest speck of dust, filling the air. They enter my body with every breath. They burrow into my lungs, tumble through my veins, tunnel deep into my muscles. They penetrate the cells of my body, stealing my life force to replicate themselves.

Grandfather once told me that the Flu bug was a foolish hunter. "It kills off its only prey," he said. "In the end, there will be no one left to get sick. Then where will the Flu bug be?" We had laughed at that. Now it wasn't so funny.

The motes are settling into my body, preparing their offensive.

Is Mother K right? Is this the future?

I hear voices, then several thuds and gasps. I hear the chain rattling. My heart is hammering. I don't know what is happening, but I do know one thing: When that door opens, I am gone.

The virulence and extreme contagiousness of Grunseth's Flu, while undeniable, has been considerably exaggerated in popular opinion. While it is true that the most casual contact with a victim is likely to produce a new infection, it is not true, as has been claimed, that the virus can pass through solid glass, endure blast furnace heat, or lie dormant for months on a doorknob. Recent studies have proven that the virus cannot survive outside the human body for more than an hour or two. It cannot pass through glass or any other solid, and it is instantly killed by temperatures over 67° Celsius.

It is true, however, that victims become contagious within hours of exposure. Experiments with pigs have demonstrated that, after first contact with the virus, they are able to transmit the disease within three to four hours.

—from *A Recent History of the Human Race* by P. D. Boggs © 2038

Part Three:

Tim

CRAZED

I WOKE UP AND HEARD BELLA talking to Ceej, her voice low and soft. I opened my eyes a crack. Her hands were on his neck, giving him a massage.

Harryette gave me a massage one time. She rubbed my shoulders for a few minutes when we were all watching a movie. I think it was *Ghostbusters*. I tried to remember her fingers digging into my neck but I kept seeing her face looking at me out that third-story window signing at me: *Go away!*

How could she want me to go away? The Kinka must have done something to her. She couldn't really not want to come with us.

I made a picture of Harryette's face in my head: Green flecks in her eyes. The corner of her mouth dimpling just before she smiled. Hands making signs, fingers forming letters, words, thoughts. *You are very agile,* she once said to me, finger spelling the word *agile.* I had to ask Ceej what it meant. He told me it was the opposite of clumsy. That made me feel good. I liked that Harryette thought I was agile. Sometimes, when she was watching, I would try to act agile.

I remembered this one time sitting in front of her

watching her hands move. She was teaching me to sign, forming thoughts in the air and putting them inside my head. Even though we were not actually touching, I could feel her.

I will feel her again soon, I thought.

I closed my eyes and saw her green eyes laughing. Her lips smiling. Her hands telling me to come closer.

After a while I fell back asleep.

I woke up with Ceej's fingers digging in, shaking me, his voice urgent in my face.

"Tim! Wake up!"

I knocked his hands away and sat up, my mind still a fog. We were in the Ranger Office. Evening sunlight filtered in through the fly-specked windows.

Ceej wore a frantic, scared look. "Bella's gone."

My first thought was, *Good!* With her gone we can get down to the business of rescuing Harryette. Then we can drive up to Page and try to do something about the dam without all this mumbo jumbo about other worlds and——But I could see that Ceej was really shook up.

"Where'd she go?" I asked.

"How do I know? I woke up and she was gone!"

"Okay, just take it easy. Maybe she went back into the canyon."

"Why would she do that?"

"To get to her sipa-whatchacallit. I dunno."

"But . . . I was going with her!" He sounded whiny, like a little kid.

I used to think if I was half as smart as Ceej I'd know twice as much as I needed. Ceej had the brains all the way. Me, I just do whatever comes into my head. That's why I got in so much trouble. I counted on Ceej to keep me from doing stupid stuff. That was why it was so weird when he went all goofy over Bella. Walking around all moon-eyed. He couldn't see she was nuts. I think he actually believed that Indian legend stuff. Like, you crawl through a hole and there's this whole Flu-free planet waiting, the Third World. Maybe the snakebite fried his brain.

Or maybe he was in love. I've seen all the movies. Love can mess a guy up way worse than snakebite.

"You're as crazy as she is," I said.

Ceej's face turned red. "She's not crazy!"

"Okay, okay, take it easy." It was my turn to be the reasonable, smart one. I stood up and looked around the room. Bella's leather pack was leaning against the end of the ratty old sofa. "She didn't take her pack. That must mean she's planning to come back."

Ceej devoured the pack with his eyes, hope naked on his face. It was a sorry sight. I turned away from him and walked into the next room.

That was when I saw her hair.

• • •

We both knew right away what she'd done. The only reason she'd have cut off all her hair was if she wanted to look like a Survivor. Maybe she'd decided to join the Kinka, or maybe she'd gone after Harryette. Either way, as far as I was concerned, it proved she was nuts.

"We gotta go after her," Ceej said, tying on his boots.

"We better wait for dark," I said. "We go out there now, they'll see us for sure."

"No they won't. Not if we're careful."

I grabbed him by the shoulders. "Just sit and think for a minute, okay? If they see us, it's all over."

He shrugged me off.

I said, "It'll be dark in an hour or so, then we can go get her and Harryette both."

Ceej sat very still for a few seconds. "She's not crazy," he said.

At least he wasn't charging outside in broad daylight. I said, "You don't really believe all that stuff about another world, do you?"

"Why not? It's no weirder than any other religion. It's no weirder than Heaven and Hell and the Garden of Eden and Noah's Ark and all that."

"Maybe, but Bella's talking about crawling down some hole in the ground."

"Her grandfather was *there*. He *saw* it."

"That's what *she* says. Look, I'm not blaming her for being kind of loopy. All that time wandering around alone in the canyon would make anybody a little strange. She thinks she can crawl down a hole and end up in paradise. And now this chopping off her hair and joining up with the Kinka——"

"She's not joining them!"

"We don't know that. We don't know *what* she's doing. But whatever it is, it's dangerous. If we're not careful we'll all end up dead."

Ceej was giving me a look, his mouth hanging open, his eyes blinking. I thought maybe I'd gotten through to him.

I said, "We can't afford any mistakes."

Ceej stood up.

"I'm going," he said, moving toward the door. "She needs me."

I stepped in front of him.

"No you're not," I said, bracing myself.

I never saw it coming. His fist connected with the point of my chin; my teeth clacked together, sending a shockwave over the top of my skull. I staggered back and hit the wall. Stunned, I slid down onto my butt, dimly aware that Ceej was opening the door and stepping outside.

It took forever for my brain to start working again. Or maybe it was only a minute. Either way, Ceej was gone and I was alone.

As I sat sorting through the fuzzies in my head I thought, I'll just take off, leave them all behind, find a safe town and set myself up nice and comfortable. Hap was dead. Emory and Harryette had joined up with the Kinka. Bella and Ceej were both bonkers. I didn't need them. I could make it on my own. Why put up with a bunch of crazies? I got up and started stuffing things in my pack. I'd head for Tusayan. Find a working car. I'd go east, toward Holbrook. There were still a few people living there—me and Hap and Emory had traded with them a few times. They were Mormons, but I was pretty sure they'd let me stay with them for a while.

But by the time I'd filled up my pack, I was thinking about Harryette again. She'd told me to go away, but I knew she didn't mean it. I kept seeing her face. I could almost count the flecks of gold in her green eyes. I remembered the way she smelled, sweet, with just a hint of vanilla, and the feel of her hands on my shoulders, and the way her hands moved, forming silent words, talking to me. The thought of never seeing her again hit me like a sharp blade twisting in my gut.

Was that how Ceej felt about Bella? Yes, I decided, only more. I tried to imagine the way I felt about Harryette multiplied ten times, but I couldn't. I couldn't leave them. Not any of them.

I grabbed the rifle and left the Ranger Office.

THE BOILER ROOM

I CAUGHT UP WITH CEEJ just down the hill from El Tovar. He was standing in the open, staring at the front entrance of the hotel. When I came up behind him he didn't even turn around.

"The least you can do is stay out of sight," I said.

Ceej shook his head. "Something's going on. They're all inside."

Just then, three Kinka came out of the lobby.

"Not anymore."

I grabbed Ceej and pulled him over a low stone wall into a locust thicket. The Kinka started down the steps to the driveway. A tall black woman in a purple robe—Mother K—followed them out the lobby door. Right behind her came Harryette, signing frantically.

Harryette was signing, *Wait, please wait.*

Mother K kept her eyes fixed straight ahead. She would not look at Harryette. Other Kinka were coming from the lobby, following them. They were all talking, their voices sounding like the putter of a distant engine. The first three—two large men on either side of a younger, smaller Kinka—were coming down the driveway. They would pass within a few feet of us. I heard a low moan—almost a growl—come from Ceej. He was staring fiercely at the three. The one in the middle, I suddenly realized, was Bella. I hadn't recognized her without her thick black hair. She was struggling. The two men held her by the arms, pulling her along against her will.

Afraid he'd run out there after her, I grabbed Ceej's arm. It was hard as granite. We could hear Bella pleading, demanding to be let go. I saw another familiar face: Emory, wearing his usual slack-jawed expression, walked slightly behind the milling, muttering crowd. Two thick blue stripes were painted across his forehead. We remained still and silent, hidden by the frilly leaves, until they had passed us by.

"Where are they going?" I whispered.

Ceej motioned for me to be quiet. The Kinka parade turned at the bottom of the hill and took the service road toward the rear of the hotel. Ceej and I left the thicket and ran across the driveway to an overgrown footpath that paralleled the service road. Hidden by a screen of pinyon pine and tall grasses, we kept pace with the Kinka, watching as they turned uphill to the paved area at the rear of the hotel.

"They're going to the old boiler room," Ceej said.

The group gathered near the door to the boiler room, a twenty-by-twenty foot, windowless, log building attached to the back of the hotel. We lost sight of Bella and Harryette behind the mass of Kinka bodies, but we could see the door open and close. The crowd let out a low sound, like forty people all sucking in their breath at the same time. Seconds later, the crowd began to break up and move back toward us. We ducked down low in the tall grass. Harryette and Mother K stayed by the boiler room with the two men who'd been holding Bella. Emory, standing off to the side, watched expressionlessly. One of the men fastened a chain to the door. Harryette suddenly ran to the door and tried to pull it open, but the other man wrestled her away and twisted her arm behind her back. Mother K stepped forward and cuffed Harryette on the side of the head and shouted something. She turned, purple robes swirling, and walked quickly back around the hotel. The man holding Harryette followed, squeezing Harryette's arm, pushing her in front of him. The other man—the one who had chained the door—sat down on the step and rested his back against the doorjamb.

We saw no sign of Bella. They had locked her in the boiler room.

Keeping our heads down, we waited for the Kinka to pass our position. After a half a minute I raised my head and found myself looking at Emory. He was standing in the driveway not thirty feet away, staring directly at us. I froze. After a few seconds, Emory shrugged and continued up the hill.

"You think he saw us?" Ceej whispered.

"Oh, yeah." One thing about Emory. He didn't miss much.

"We better get out of here."

I shook my head. "He won't say anything." Somehow I knew it was true. I'd known Emory for a long time.

A few minutes later I caught a familiar smell. Cigar smoke. I couldn't be sure, but I would've bet anything it was one of Hap's cigars. I raised my head and saw a cloud of transparent blue smoke hanging over the guard. In his fingers was a short, black cigar. A surge of anger blasted up my spine—I wanted to run at him and grab that cigar out of his hand and grind it in his face.

Ceej held me back. It was *his* turn keep *me* from doing something stupid.

"Wait for dark," he said.

"I know."

"She has to be in there," Ceej said. "She's got to be."

I agreed with him, but my mind wasn't on Bella. I was worried about Harryette. I didn't like the way she'd been dragged off. "We'll get both of them, Bella and Harryette, after dark. Okay?"

Ceej agreed. "Before the moon rises."

Hap always told me that simple plans are the best. "You get yourself all tangled up if you get too smart," he once told me. "Best way to get from here to there, you start walkin'. That's the way you do it, boy. You pick your time and place, and you act."

I'd been trying real hard not to think about Hap.

Shortly after sunset, while the sky was still light, a teenaged Kinka with yellow circles painted on his face brought a plate of food to the Kinka guarding the boiler room. That reminded me of how hungry I was, but we didn't have any food with us. I stripped a blade of grass and put it in my mouth for something to chew on.

I hate waiting more than anything.

We watched the Kinka eat his food. By the time he finished it was almost dark. We heard the rumble of the generator start up, and a few lights came on inside El Tovar. The Kinka lit another cigar. The smell drifted toward us.

"Let's go," I said.

Moving silently, we left the thicket. I approached the boiler room from the east side, while Ceej came around to the opposite side of the building. Ceej had the rifle. I gave him thirty seconds to get into position, then stepped around the corner of the building.

"Hey, ugly."

The Kinka dropped the cigar and jumped to his feet, startled. He was about twice as big as I'd thought. "Who the——"

Ceej stepped around the far corner of the building, took two long strides and swung the rifle like a baseball bat. Gun stock glanced off naked scalp; the Kinka staggered and let out a ragged gasp. I ran at him and drove my shoulder into his side. It was like running into a boulder. With a roar of fury, the Kinka grabbed my arm and threw me against the side of the building. I saw Ceej swinging the rifle again, chopping down with it. If it had been an ax, it would've split that Kinka's skull straight down the middle. The Kinka dropped to his knees, dazed. He shook his head and started to rise, and I took another run at him, this time driving my fist, all my weight behind it, into his nose. His head snapped back, but he still didn't go down. I tried to hit him again, but suddenly his arms were around me and he was on top of me, breathing cigar breath in my face, squeezing the air from my lungs. I heard a soft thud, and his grip loosened. Another thud. Something hot and wet spilled across my face. The Kinka made a whimpering sound. Another thud, and he was dead weight on top of me. I pushed and kicked my way out from under him and saw Ceej's face white in the faint starlight, saw him raise the rifle to swing it again.

I jumped up and grabbed the gun from Ceej. "It's okay, he's out," I said. The rifle stock was black and sticky with blood—I was glad it was too dark to see its redness. "You get Bella, I'll stand guard." I ran a few yards down the short path to where I could see anyone coming from the direction of the hotel. I heard Ceej struggling with the chain, then the clatter of links being pulled free. I turned to look just as the door crashed open and a dark figure came boiling out, knocking Ceej down, dashing down the hill and into the woods.

Ceej yelled, "Bella, wait!" He took off after her.

I stood there for a few seconds, not sure what to do. Bella running away hadn't been part of our plan. Should I go after them? I waited a minute, undecided. Ceej and I had agreed that if we somehow got split up, we would meet back at the Ranger Office, but going back to the Ranger Office now didn't seem like such a good idea. The unconscious Kinka might wake up any time now, or another Kinka might come to relieve him. Once the Kinka knew we were around, they'd search all the nearby buildings in a hurry.

No time to lose. Ceej would catch up to Bella, or he wouldn't. We would have to find each other later at our back-up rendezvous. It was time to act.

Gripping the bloody rifle, I started up the hill toward El Tovar.

That was when I heard the first cough.

I stopped, trying to locate the sound. After a few seconds it came again, a liquid rattle that made the hairs on my neck stand up.

It was coming from inside the boiler room.

I took a few steps back, toward the open door.

More coughing. Deep, gurgling, lung-shredding, agonizing, virus-spewing explosions. I stood ten feet back from the door, staring into the black rectangle. All my instincts told me to run, to get as far away from this house of death as my legs could carry me. But something else held me rooted there.

"Hello?" I called out.

The coughing stopped. I heard the sound of air being sucked in and out of ravaged lungs, then a familiar voice, hoarse and twisted with pain.

"Boy, you come one step closer you die."

"Dad?"

"You ever listen to me, boy, you—" More coughing. "—you listen now. *Go away!*"

I saw something move, dark on dark, then the door swung shut and the coughing started up again, now muffled. I felt my belly clench and twist inside me and it was all I could do not to fall to the ground in a miserable knot. A part of me wanted to rush into that boiler room. I didn't care if I got sick and died. Life was too hard and lonely. But another part of me wanted to take off into the woods, to turn off my brain and live like an animal on berries and squirrels, drinking water from puddles and sleeping in the pine duff.

I don't know how long I stood there with my eyes squeezed shut. Maybe only a few seconds. Then I remembered Harryette looking out that window. I remembered her eyes and her hands, and I found myself walking up the hill toward El Tovar. I found an empty place in my head and I put the boiler room there. I would think about it another time, I promised myself.

But not now. I still had something to live for.

EL TOVAR

THE IRON LADDER BUILT ONTO THE canyon side of El Tovar was rusted and missing a few rungs. I'd been up and down it before, but each time it got a little scarier. I'd need both hands, so I unloaded the rifle, ran my belt through the trigger guard, hung it over my shoulder and started to climb. The ladder gave off a few heart-stopping creaks, and one of the bolts that held it to the side of the building popped off as I climbed by, but I made it to the top. I stepped off the ladder onto cedar shingles spongy from years of neglect—carpenter ants, mold, and mildew had taken the starch out of them. I walked carefully. There were places so rotten that your foot would go right through.

El Tovar's roof was shaped like a barn roof—gently sloped on top, and steep at the sides. Each third-floor room had its own gable window jutting from the steep part of the roof. All I had to do was pick out the room where I'd seen Harryette the night before, work my way around the gable, and drop down onto the narrow ledge outside the window. It sounded easy, but it had to be a one-way trip. Once I got on the ledge there was no way I could get back up. But I didn't figure to be retreating. I just hoped I wouldn't fall off the roof and kill myself. And I hoped the window wouldn't be stuck shut, and that I picked the right room, and that Harryette would be there, and she'd be alone, and—*no!* I had to quit thinking like Ceej, sweating all the details.

No more thinking. Time to act.

Following the ridge of the roof, I made my way to a point above the third gable from the north end and slid carefully down, aiming one foot at each side of the gable peak until I was sitting astride it. I inched my way out to the edge of the gable, leaned out over the eaves and looked down into the window below. The room was dark. If Harryette was there, she was sitting in the dark. I don't remember making the decision, but the next instant my bottom half was hanging over the edge of the gable roof, feeling for the ledge below.

It was farther down than I had thought—my feet found only open space. I hung there, fingers digging into rotten shingle. I knew the ledge was there, but was it a few inches or a few feet below? The sill was only about ten inches wide. If I landed wrong, I could fall the entire three stories.

The decision was made for me when the shingles ripped loose. I fell, my hands shot out and clawed glass, my feet hit something solid, and I was on the ledge, my heart banging. For several seconds I didn't move, getting used to the idea that I was still alive.

I was pretty sure that no one was in the room, or they'd be looking out at me. I found the edge of the window with my fingers and tried to pull it open. I couldn't pull too hard—if I gave it a really hard yank and it came open suddenly, I'd be on my way down to the ground the fast way. I wasted a few minutes trying to pry it open with my pocket-knife, but busted the tip off the blade. Only one thing to do. I unslung the rifle and slammed the butt into the glass pane. The glass shattered with a horrendously loud sound. I knocked away the shards, reached in and unlatched the window. It swung open easily. I climbed inside. The room was empty, but I knew right away that I had the right room. Her scent still hung in the air. I opened the door and stuck my head out into the hallway, half-expecting hordes of Kinka to come rushing at me.

The hallway was dark and empty and quiet. I made my way past the other rooms, walking close to the wall so the floor wouldn't creak. As I approached the staircase I heard voices coming from below. I went down the stairs to the second floor. Now I heard a single voice, coming from the direction of the mezzanine. I walked silently down the carpeted hallway. The voice was coming from the lobby. I got down on my hands and knees and crawled as I reached the mezzanine, the open area that overlooked the lobby. I could see the orange flickering of firelight tickling the wood beams of the lobby walls and ceiling.

The voice rose and fell and became a stream of words.

"*. . . and the evil spread. Women abandoned their children.*

Men beat their wives. The leaders of the nations of the world told lies to each other, and lied to their own people, and lied to themselves . . ."

I got down on my belly and wriggled up to the railing at the edge of the mezzanine and peeked through the wooden posts. The lobby was packed with Kinka—dozens of them sitting on the floor, on the furniture, on each other. They were listening, their eyes reflecting firelight. Mother K, now wearing a long golden robe, stood before the roaring fireplace. She spoke in a hypnotic, singsong rhythm. I had the feeling she had spoken these same words many times before.

". . . and the evil spread. Children joined gangs, they soiled their bodies with drugs, they killed one another with knives and bullets and cars. And the religions of the world became muddled and soft, and God was forgotten by his priests and ministers. And there were wars and famines and floods and storms and earthquakes and plagues, and many people died, but always there were more babies born, and they were stained with the evil of their parents."

She spread her arms wide, the golden robe unfurling like great wings.

"Hear me now. Listen to Mother K. Evil fell like a mist over the land, and people saw it but only blinked it away and shrugged and said, 'It is only the smog.'"

The Kinka swayed back and forth, lost in firelight and words. The melody and rhythm of the woman's voice made me want to be down there with them, mindless and swaying. Then I saw Harryette sitting back by the wall beneath Bullwinkle's moth-eaten beard. The words must have been gibberish to her, but she was listening as intently as the rest of them. Even Bullwinkle the moose seemed to be listening.

If I was ever going to get her away from the Kinka, it would have to be soon.

"Then one day, when the evil had become too much for the land to bear, the hand of God reached down from heaven and touched a man. And that man touched other men, and the hand of God spread, a purifying flame, throughout the land. And men and women and children fell, cleansed of life. The people of Earth, soiled by greed and wickedness, were dying."

She bowed her head, and all the other Kinka bowed their heads as well. For a moment the crackling of the fire was the only sound.

"But then, by God's mercy, Survivors began to appear. A young man in New York. A girl in Los Angeles. In Kansas City, in Flagstaff, in Seattle there were those blessed few who were touched but lightly by the hand of God. All over the world, Survivors began to appear. You, and you, and you—"

She pointed randomly at faces amongst the Kinka.

"—are the chosen. You, all of you, have within you a pure, clean, untainted place in your soul. God has chosen you to Survive. As God chose Noah and his children millennia ago, so have you been chosen to inherit this world. It is our destiny to spread the touch of God to all, so that every man, woman, and child is subject to the Judgment of the Divine.

"We are the Kinka. We are the chosen . . ."

THE JUDGMENT OF THE DIVINE

I HAD BEEN WAITING FOR MORE than an hour in the closet in Harryette's room when the door finally opened and the light came on. I held my breath, looking out through the half-open closet door. I saw Harryette's profile as she stepped into the room. She stopped and looked around the room, her brow wrinkled, sensing that something was different. I wanted to let her know I was there, but not until I was sure we were alone.

She took a few more steps, walking right up to the window. I had closed the curtains to cover up the shattered glass. If she opened them she would know right away that someone had broken in.

I heard the soft tread of another person entering the room and saw the golden robes of the Kinka leader.

"What is wrong, child?" she asked.

Harryette turned at the sound of the Kinka's voice. Her hands jerked, like she'd been about to sign something but had realized that it wouldn't be understood.

"You are disturbed by the girl, aren't you?" said the Kinka. She closed the door, sat down on the edge of the bed and patted the mattress beside her. "Come, sit with Mother K."

Harryette sat down beside Mother K.

"It is a most difficult thing, to watch the old race die." She lifted one of Harryette's hands and began to stroke it. "We must be strong. It is the Judgment of the Divine." She pulled Harryette's hand to her chest. "Feel my heart beat. It beats for you. All of us are here for you."

Harryette stared back at Mother K.

"You don't understand me, do you, child?" She released Harryette's hand and, looking into her eyes, clumsily made the signs for *family*, *love*, and *friend*.

Harryette nodded. This she understood. Her eyes filled with tears.

I couldn't wait any longer. I stepped out of the closet and stuck the rifle in Mother K's face, right between her golden eyes.

I don't know what I expected. If somebody had pointed a gun at my face I don't think I would have smiled and stood up and introduced myself. But that was exactly what Mother K did. She even held out her hand, like she expected me to shake it or kiss it or something.

"Lie down on the floor, face down!" I said, quoting some cop movie I'd seen.

Mother K laughed.

"You better do it now or I'll shoot you."

"I do not fear your weapon."

Harryette, still sitting on the bed, was signing frantically, *Don't shoot her!*

Mother K's smile broadened, like she knew there was no way I'd do it. But she was wrong. I thumbed back the hammer. She must have sensed something, because her smile faded slightly.

"Now, child, there's no reason for you to be so upset," she said.

"I'm no child, and you better do what I say. Lie down!"

Mother K tipped her head like a fox listening for a field mouse. Her eyes lost focus. "But he says he will shoot me," she said. She frowned and nodded. "Alright then." She backed up until her legs hit the bed, then slowly sank onto the mattress and crossed her hands on her lap.

"How about if we just sit here with Miss Harryette?" she said, her smile returning.

I shook my head. I needed both hands to talk to Harryette, and I didn't dare let go of the gun as long as this Kinka woman could make a dash for the door.

"You will be judged," said Mother K. "It is only a matter of time. Why wait?"

I stepped into her and put the gun barrel to her chest and gave a vicious shove. Mother K fell back with a gasp. Harryette jumped up. For a moment I thought she was going to throw herself between Mother K and the gun, but she just stood there looking frantically from me to Mother K and back again. Mother K's eyes were huge, her golden irises surrounded by white. At least she was taking me seriously now.

"Roll over," I said.

She hesitated, then turned onto her belly. "They say you are dangerous, they say I must do as you say," she said.

"Who are 'they'?" I asked.

"My friends and enemies."

I leaned the rifle against the dressing table, grabbed the edge of the bedspread, and threw it over her, then rolled her up like a burrito.

Harryette signed, *What are you doing!*

Helping you escape, I signed back.

You can't. They'll come after us.

They won't catch us. I pulled out the coil of rope I'd stashed under the bed. I'd found the rope in the first floor utility closet while Mother K was brainwashing her troops. I cut off a few feet, and wrapped it around Mother K's ankles.

I won't go.

You have to.

No! If you leave now, I'll try to keep her from going after you.

Like you saved Bella?

Who?

I made the signs for *Native American* and *girl.*

Harryette set her jaw. *I tried to help her!*

I tied the rope, then cut another length and wrapped it around Mother K's arms and shoulders. All that time, Mother K was talking, but her words were muffled by layers of cotton and wool. She looked like a giant cocoon.

I tied one end of the coil of rope around the leg of the radiator and dropped the other end out the window. Harryette was staring at me intently, her brow furrowed. I could not imagine what she was thinking, but I knew what we had to do.

Now let's get out of here, I signed, pointing at the window.

She shook her head.

I signed, *I am not leaving until you do.*

If you stay they'll catch you. She looked at the cocooned form of Mother K. *You'll be judged.*

I nodded. *Then that is what will happen.*

Harryette closed her eyes. Her face twisted, like something was hurting her. Then she opened her eyes. She had made her decision.

Climbing down thirty feet of rope seemed like it should be easy, but the nylon rope was thin and hard to grip. I showed Harryette how to wrap it around her wrists and ankles and, slowly, she made her way down to the ground. Once she was down, I pulled the rope up, tied the rifle to the end, and lowered it to the ground, then followed, rappelling quickly down the side of the building.

Now what? she asked. *Where is Ceej?*

I don't know. We crossed the circular driveway, then

ran down the short hill to where the Land Rover and Jeep were parked. So far, no one had raised the alarm, but I wasn't sure how long the cocoon would hold Mother K. Popping open the Land Rover's hood, I grabbed a handful of plug wires, ripped them loose, and threw them into the weeds.

I motioned Harryette to get into the Jeep. I jumped in behind the wheel. The keys weren't in the ignition, but that was no surprise. Hap always kept a spare set stashed in the door pocket. I reached for them. My heart stopped. A bubble of fear filled my chest.

What's wrong? Harryette asked.

No keys. We have to run. I opened the door, grabbed the rifle, and got out.

Then I saw a figure watching us from the edge of the driveway. Blue paint crusted his scalp. He raised one arm. A set of keys dangled from his thick fingers.

"Emory," I said. The rifle felt heavy in my hands.

"You should not have come back here," he rumbled.

Harryette got out of the other side of the Jeep.

Emory looked at her, blinking.

"You wish to leave us, Harryette?" he said, pointing at her, then off into the darkness.

Harryette nodded again, understanding his meaning.

Emory pursed his full lips, staring at her. His eyes shifted to me. "Your father, he was a good man," he said.

I wondered if I could shoot him. Emory, divining my thoughts, looked down at the gun in my hands. "It is inevitable," he said, his hands closing around the keys.

Excited voices erupted inside the hotel. They had found Mother K, or she had worked herself free.

Emory, looking toward the hotel, said, "It will come to pass."

The front door of El Tovar crashed open and a dozen Kinka flooded out into the night. One of them spotted us and shouted, and suddenly they were running toward us. Emory remained still for a heartbeat, his usually slack features contorting with indecision, then he jumped into the driver's seat and rammed the key into the ignition.

"Get in," he said, twisting the key. Harryette and I scrambled into the Jeep as the engine roared to life. "Stay down," he ordered. With a squeal of spinning tires, we hurtled down the driveway toward the rim road.

"All right, Emory!" I shouted, looking back at the horde of pursuing Kinka. Emory reached across the seat and palmed my head and pushed it down just as the back window exploded, sending a spray of glass through the cab. I heard two more shots, and then we rounded a bend and were out of range. I sat up. Harryette was lying on the back seat looking up at me, eyes wide.

"We're clear," I said to Emory, giving Harryette a

thumbs-up. "I yanked the plug wires on the Land Rover. They'll never catch us."

Emory didn't slow down. "They have motor-cycles," he said.

"They do?" It was the first I knew anything about motorcycles.

"They will be coming."

In the distance, I heard the whine of a motorcycle engine. "They'd better not get too close." I raised the rifle and pointed it out the back window, but Emory ripped it from my grasp.

"Hey!"

"I will take you where you wish to go," said Emory. "But you will injure no one." He threw the rifle out the window.

"But they—"

"Where do you wish to go?"

"We have to find Ceej."

"Where?"

"I don't know. But we decided that if we got sepa-rated we'd meet up at Desert View."

Emory nodded. "I will take you to Desert View."

I could hear two motorcycle engines now, one a high-pitched whine, the other a throaty roar. Just past the turnoff to Tusayan, Emory let up on the gas, cranked the wheel to the right, and turned onto an old service road. The Jeep bounced along the rutted, overgrown trail for a few dozen yards, then stopped, just out of sight of the road. Emory shut off the engine and lights.

"We sit here quiet now," he said.

The motorcycles passed by and kept going until we couldn't hear them at all. We listened to the faint pings and creaks of the Jeep's engine cooling. Minutes later we heard the bikes again, this time heading back toward the village.

"All right," Emory said. "Since they did not catch up with us on the rim road, they will think we are headed for Tusayan." He backed the Jeep out to the road and pointed it east, shifted into first gear, and we were on our way.

I spent most of the drive to Desert View trying to bring Harryette up to speed. I turned on the dome light so we could talk with our hands.

And then what? she asked. *If Ceej shows up, then what?*

There is still the dam, I signed. *We have to get to Page.*

Emory must have understood some of our silent conversation, because he said, "It is of little use, young one. The dam will fail. Mother K has foretold this."

"Mother K is the *cause* of it," I said.

Emory shook his head slowly. "You do not understand. But your time will come. Perhaps you will be judged fit to join us."

"Not if I can help it."

Emory's lips stretched across his big front teeth and he began to make a huffing sound. For a moment I thought he was choking, then I realized it was laughter. I had never heard Emory laugh before.

"What's so funny?"

He shook his head. "You make me believe you."

"You should come with us."

"No, I do not think so."

"Then why are you helping us?"

Emory drove in silence for several seconds, then said, "Your father was a good man. He would have wanted me to help you."

"You can't go back. They'll know you helped us get away."

"They will not harm me. They are my people."

"They sure harmed Hap."

Emory's face contorted; his hands tightened on the steering wheel. "You do not understand. Your father was given to the Judgment of the Divine. There was no intent to harm him."

"Yeah, well, it did."

Emory looked at me for so long I was afraid he'd drive off the road. Finally he looked away and did not say another word until we reached Desert View.

Standing beneath the dark bulk of the Watchtower, we watched the Jeep's taillights disappear. Emory said he would keep driving the thirty miles to Cameron, then circle back through Tusayan and return to Grand Canyon Village. He said he'd tell the rest of the Kinka that we had forced him to drive us to Flagstaff. We were safe, for the time being. The air temperature suddenly seemed to drop, and I could hear the wind rushing up the walls of the canyon. A cold front moving in?

I looked at Harryette. She stood with her eyes closed, hugging herself, looking as small and frail as I felt.

What now? she signed.

I looked up at the ragged stone walls.

We wait for Ceej.

THE WATCHTOWER

THE WATCHTOWER AT DESERT VIEW is a cylindrical stone building sticking up seventy feet above the canyon rim. It was built a hundred years ago as a scenic view for tourists. Ceej had suggested the tower as our backup rendezvous. He and his uncle had hidden caches of food, water, and survival gear at several places in and around Grand Canyon. "Just in case," Ceej's uncle had said. "Because you never know what might happen someday."

This was someday, and the Watchtower concealed one of those caches.

Harryette and I found the metal footlocker hidden beneath a pile of broken furniture on the first floor of the Watchtower. I pried it open. The first thing I felt was a flashlight. I pressed the switch and a weak yellow glow illuminated the cache: several glass jugs of water, boxes and bags of food, a shotgun, a medical kit, and some blankets. I was mostly interested in the food—the excitement of the past few hours had made me ravenous. I pointed the flashlight at my face and moved my left hand from my mouth toward my stomach.

Hungry?

Harryette nodded. I got out one of the water jugs and a box of Raisin Bran. I turned off the flashlight to save what little was left of the batteries. We sat down on the stone floor and ate handfuls of cereal and washed it down with water. No one had made Raisin Bran since before the Flu, so this box had to be more than ten years old. The raisins were hard as old pine resin, but sweet as candy. We ate like starving animals, shoving food into our mouths like we'd never eat again.

We felt our way up the winding staircase, blankets draped over our shoulders, hands sliding up the rawhide-wrapped banister, invisible spider webs dragging across our faces. The flashlight died halfway up the first flight. We climbed into blackness until the stairs ended. We were on the top floor. I looked out one of the small windows. On a clear day you could see a hundred miles, but on that dark night we saw only a faint brightness in the east where the moon would soon rise. The south wall of the tower was still warm from sucking up sunlight all day. We spread the blankets on the floor along the wall and sat down to wait. Assuming that Ceej and Bella were okay, it would take a few hours for them to walk all the way from the village to Desert View. We probably wouldn't see them until morning.

If they didn't show up then, I didn't know what we'd do. I didn't want to think about it. There were a lot of things I didn't want to think about. I've always been good at not thinking about things. I'm more of a doer. For instance, I had hardly thought about Hap at all. I'd put him away someplace inside my head. That's what you have to do sometimes when people die and you aren't ready for it. I was sitting with my back to the warm wall staring into blackness not thinking about Hap and Ceej and the Kinka when I felt Harryette's hand touch my shoulder, then move down my arm to my hand.

She was sitting in front of me, I could see her shape but nothing else. Her fingers wrapped my hand, lifted it to a place halfway between us. She felt for my other hand, found it, and brought it up to join the first. She held my hands there, a few inches apart, then let go and placed both of her hands between mine so that my hands were lightly touching hers. At first I didn't know what she was doing, then her hands started to move and I understood that she was talking to me.

I followed her hands with my fingers, trying to imagine the shapes they formed.

She was saying, *Thank you.*

For what?

*For taking me away from—*She tapped her forehead with the K sign. I understood her to mean the Kinka.

A huge weight lifted off me, and I knew for the first time how afraid I had been that she would hate me for taking her away.

I signed back, *I was afraid you wouldn't come.*

I did not want you to be in danger.

I don't care about that.

You are very brave.

I just wanted you to come with us.

She didn't reply, but I knew what she was thinking: Come with you where?

To change the subject I asked, *The Kinka, are they all insane?*

They are not insane. They are people. They are kind to their children. I might have stayed with them.

That Mother K, she's got to be crazy. She was listening to voices in her head!

That is her burden. All the Kinka have been hurt by the Flu. It is what brings them together.

She had strange eyes.

Yes. She is strange. We are all strange. Strange is different from insane.

Our hands filled the blackness between us. She would sign, and my hands would follow hers, and then I would sign, feeling her fingers lightly touching mine. At times it seemed we were both signing at once, sending and receiving with the speed of thought. I was hand-talking, but another part of me swam in the world of touch, surrounded by Harryette.

My hands formed the thought: *You are not strange to me.*

A faint rectangle of light appeared on the wall. Moon-rise. I could see the curve of Harryette's cheek, closer than I'd thought. She was smiling. Her nose was only inches from mine. The light got brighter as the moon mounted the horizon. Harryette brought her hands up to my face. I could feel each of her fingers, separate and distinct, hot on my cheeks, then sliding around to the back of my head, pulling me toward her.

The Flu itself must be considered the greatest disaster ever visited upon the human race, both because of the sheer number of virus-induced fatalities, and because of the hundreds of lesser disasters that followed in its wake, including three nuclear power plant meltdowns, the great fires in Manhattan and Detroit, the widespread looting and rioting in every major city, and the collapse of the Internet. Most estimates place the number of non-Flu fatalities from 2029–34 at more than three hundred million, far more than might be considered "normal."

—from *A Recent History of the Human Race* by P. D. Boggs © 2038

PART FOUR:

HARRYETTE

SORROW

MY MOTHER'S COOL HAND on my fevered forehead, tears shining on her cheeks, blue eyes fierce. I cough, spraying her with virus, both of us knowing that it was the end. And it was, for her and for Dad, but for some reason I survived and became a hairless mute.

Had I offered my parents the Judgment of the Divine, or had I simply killed them?

Something touched my arm. I opened my eyes. A circular room of stone; the Watchtower. Gray light oozed in through clouded windows, eight of them, one at each point of the compass. Morning light. Cool air prickled my scalp. I turned my head and saw Tim's face.

He smiled, greeting me with his eyes.

I nodded, seeing echoes of his father, Hap, in Tim's elfin features. The late Hap Gordon. You could sometimes tell, according to Mother K, which ones would live and which would die. Those destined to survive the Judgment always slipped into a coma a day or two after symptoms first appeared. The ones who remained conscious, fighting the virus until they were too weak to breathe, were certain to die. Both Hap and Uncle had been fighters. Grief plucked at my ribs, twisted my insides.

Tim's hand gripped mine, pulling me up into a sitting position. I was wrapped in wool. I thought of Mother K trapped in her cocoon and quickly threw off the blanket.

Tim pointed to his mouth. *Hungry?* Most of Tim's signs were ones he'd invented, but we communicated well enough. I nodded.

Tim made us breakfast of decade-old crackers with dried apples and pine nut butter. I wished we had something hot to drink, but I knew we couldn't make a fire. The Kinka probably would not look for us here—Emory would tell them we had gone off in the other direction—but the slightest curl of smoke could give us away. We had to be careful. We washed the stale crackers down with stale water. Tim ate like an animal, shoving the food into his mouth faster than he could chew. When he finished, he went and stood looking out the southwest window, waiting for Ceej.

He looked at me and moved his hands. *Ceej here soon.*

Tim's signing was clumsy and abrupt, but I knew what he meant. I nodded, smiling to show that I understood. He turned back to the window. I chewed another cracker and watched him watching. He stood very straight, his shoulders square, his feet planted firmly. Tim was always ready to move—to duck or run or charge forward. His body did what he wanted. In another time, another place, he would have been a gymnast or a soccer player. He would have been a professional athlete and I would have been a famous actress with long blond hair and a beautiful voice.

I joined him at the window looking down at the twisted ribbon of crumbling asphalt that was East Rim Drive. I put my hands on his shoulders, felt his muscles tense, then relax. I wrapped my arms around his chest and hugged, thinking that this was not so bad. We had food, we had water, we had each other. A few hours ago I had planned to spend the rest of my life with the Kinka. Now my life would go a different way.

Sometimes life takes big, sudden turns. Mine has taken several. The biggest one was when I caught the Flu, eight years ago.

I remember the pain, the coughing, and knowing I would die. I was both frightened and sad. I remember the coma taking me, sucking me deep into its black embrace. I must have been gone a long time. Later, Ceej told me that it had been a week, but he was only eight years old and probably exaggerating. I woke up in a strange bed, hungry and thirsty and confused. I looked into the mirror hanging on the wall and saw a pale, thin, hairless creature. I tried to scream, but all that came out was a sound like fingernails clawing a blackboard. I tottered on weak legs to the doorway and looked out into an unfamiliar hallway.

There was a very bad smell in the house.

I found my mother curled up on a paisley print sofa. I did not need to touch her to know she was dead. I ran out of the house. Our Land Cruiser sat parked in the driveway. My father was behind the wheel. I ran up to him and put my hand on the door handle and pulled, but the door was locked. I put my face to the glass and saw his protruding tongue and his dry eyes. He had joined my mother.

I was sure that I would find Ceej next. I went into the house next door and found a bottle of ginger ale and a box of Oreos. I took them outside and sat on the front steps and started to eat slowly, one tiny bite at a time. I was halfway through the box of cookies when Ceej came strolling down the street. I thought I was dreaming.

He saw me a second after I saw him. He walked up to me. His mouth opened and sounds came out. They sounded like words, but in some strange foreign language. I tried to ask, "What did you say?" but when I pushed the words from my brain toward my mouth, nothing happened.

I had forgotten how to talk.

Since then I've read a lot about the way the brain works, but nothing I've read comes close to explaining what happened to me while I was in that coma. The one thing I've learned is the more you know about the human brain, the more strange and mysterious it gets. I've read about a man who was perfectly normal except that he couldn't recognize his own face. I've read about people who can see sounds and smell colors. I've read about a woman who ate her own children, and about a man who ate an entire Volkswagen. What happened to me was no stranger than that. At least I knew who I was. At least I wasn't eating a car.

But it was terrible. I felt cut off from Ceej, as if a wall of glass brick surrounded me. For months, or maybe years, I was sure that one day I would wake up and words would pour from my mouth. It hasn't happened. Fortunately, I could still read and write. And I could learn to sign. I was better off than many Survivors who lost their eyesight or hearing, or both, or who had gone completely insane. But the wall was still there.

During the days I had spent with the Kinka, I learned that I was not alone. Every Survivor is damaged. Some, like Emory, seem normal at first—but the Flu changes all who are exposed. Emory had been an artist before he got sick. He had painted fantastic scenes of starships and other planets, but after the Flu, he discovered that he had lost his ability to dream, and to create. When he touched pencil to paper he saw nothing, he imagined nothing. Emory was the saddest of men.

Mother K, who could see and hear and speak with perfect clarity, had lost her ability to be alone. While I could not understand a single spoken word, Mother K was constantly bombarded by voices inside her head, demanding her attention. Some of the voices she could ignore; others were more insistent.

All of us had been damaged. All of us were alone. But as Kinka, we had been alone together. Together we were a whole. Such was Mother K's message, and the Kinka's lure.

But now I was with Tim, and I would stay with him. Of all the people I knew, Tim came the closest to penetrating the glass wall. He was a terrible signer, but his hands moved with such urgency and eagerness that I always knew what he was trying to say. The bond between us was stronger than anything the Kinka had to offer.

Ceej showed up a couple of hours later, trudging down the rim road. He was not alone. At first, I thought the person walking beside him was Kinka. Then I recognized the girl, the false Kinka.

The one who had been judged.

Tim shouted from the window. Ceej looked up and waved wearily. He and the girl walked to a low stone wall and sat down. Tim started for the stairs, but I grabbed him and made him look at me.

She is not safe, I signed. *She is sick with Flu!*

His shoulders sagged, and I saw that he believed me. *Like Hap.*

You know about Hap?

Tim nodded. *We talked.*

You talked to him? I was afraid to ask the next question, but I had to. *How close did you get to him?*

Not close. He told me to go away. He was sick.

Then you know that the girl is infected.

Tim nodded, his face contorted. I wasn't telling him anything he didn't know, but I had to say it.

Now Ceej is infected, too.

THE COUGH

CEEJ, BELLA, AND I SAT ON the low wall surrounding the
stone patio at the base of the tower. Tim stayed fifty
feet away and upwind. Until we knew for sure
whether Bella had caught the disease, he would have
to keep his distance.

As for Ceej, I had little hope. If it was too late for
Bella, it was too late for him.

Talking and signing, Ceej told us what happened
after they freed Bella.

Bella had come rushing out, knocking Ceej down
and running off into the woods. She had been so
scared she hadn't even realized it was him. Ceej took
off after her but, with his sore foot, he wasn't fast
enough. He had stumbled around in the dark forest,
calling her name as loud as he dared.

Bella, meanwhile, had circled back to the Ranger
Office. When Ceej finally thought to go back there
himself, he found Bella sitting in the darkness on the
front steps wearing her backpack. That was about the
same time things busted loose at El Tovar. Ceej and
Bella heard engines, then shouting, then saw lights
flashing. They didn't know if her escape had been

discovered, or if Tim had been caught, or if something else had happened, but they knew it was time to leave. They'd started walking toward Desert View. They'd walked all night. I could see the fatigue in their eyes and in the way they sat on the low stone wall, leaning against each other for support.

Why did you let him near you? I asked Bella. I was too angry to care if she understood me. *You knew you'd been exposed!*

She stared at my moving hands, uncomprehending.

Ceej answered, giving me his defiant, stubborn, little-brother stare. *It doesn't make any difference.*

How can you say that? Do you want to die?

Ceej stared back at me, blinking as if I had signed gibberish. He whispered something to Bella. She sat up straighter and spoke to me, her expression intent and earnest.

Ceej interpreted, speaking and signing. *She says that she is sorry that you are angry with her. She says that it is possible she has the Flu, but it does not matter, as long as we make it to the*—Ceej finger spelled a word I'd never seen—*Sipapuni.*

The what?

Ceej frowned, thinking. *It is a place*—

Bella began to speak. When she spoke, her eyes became larger and fixed upon me with an intensity that reminded me of Mother K. Ceej's hands moved, translating. *It is a holy place, the place of emergence. She is the last of her people*—He stopped signing and asked

Bella a question. She replied. He continued, —*the last Hopi. She is traveling to the Sipapuni to rejoin her people*—

You said she was the last one.

Yes, the last Hopi on this world.

Wait a minute. I could hardly believe what I was hearing. *Are you saying she wants to go to this place to die?*

Ceej frowned. *Who said anything about dying?*

Then what are you talking about?

Patiently, as if I were a little kid, Ceej told me a story about how the Hopi people had come into this world. Sometimes he would consult with Bella, who would speak gibberish to me, and then Ceej would translate. It sounded like a fairy tale, a Hopi myth, but Ceej told it as if he really believed it was true. I had to remind myself that this was the same little brother who thought he'd seen a ghost just a couple of weeks ago. I looked back at Tim, who shrugged, pointed at his temple and made his finger go in a circle.

I'm not crazy, Ceej said, looking very serious. *And neither is Bella. It's true. The Sipapuni is real. It will take us to the Third World. It will make us whole again. Evil cannot pass from one world to the next, and the Flu is the ultimate evil. Once we reach the other side, the Flu will no longer be with us.*

I gaped at him. I could hardly believe that he was serious.

It is our only hope, he said. He wrapped his arms around Bella.

• • •

From the top of the Watchtower, looking to the northeast, we could see up-canyon, past the sheer cliff walls called the Palisades of the Desert, all the way to Cape Solitude, where the Grand Canyon meets the Little Colorado Gorge. The gorge itself was a ragged cut in the plateau.

Tim said, *That's where they're going.* He pointed at the Little Colorado Gorge, ten miles away. Beyond it lay miles of rocky, brush-dotted wasteland and, on the horizon, the Painted Desert. To the east, between us and the gorge, stood the green, flat-topped cone known as Cedar Mountain. It was a forbidding landscape, a region as awful as it was awesome.

I said to Tim, *Can we talk them out of it?*

He shook his head.

If Mother K was floating a few inches off the ground, my brother and his new girlfriend were living on the moon. They actually believed that they were going to visit some other world, like Alice going down the rabbit hole to Wonderland. The more they explained it, the nuttier it sounded. They planned to walk ten miles to the Little Colorado, climb down into the gorge, then find this mythical hole that would take them to Wonderland, or Nirvana, or the Third World, or whatever, and would somehow in the process screen out all the Flu virus from their bodies.

I looked down at the patio at the base of the tower where Bella and Ceej were sitting. They were talking, their faces inches apart.

Tim said, *They're going to die, aren't they?*

I hesitated. Nothing I could say would make it easier. *She was in the boiler room for a long time.*

Tim stared back at me, pain in his eyes. *What are we going to do?* he asked.

Below us, Ceej laughed. He looked happy. He wasn't thinking about Uncle, or about the Kinka, or about the Flu. He might be dead soon, but today his head was filled with Bella. I felt something bubble up inside me. Envy? Jealousy? I did not know.

I said, *We have to go with them.* Tim nodded, but I wasn't sure he completely understood, so I added, *I may have to take care of them. When they get sick.*

Over the years the old Jeep trails had been washed out, overgrown, or buried in drifts of sand. Using Bella's grand-father's maps and a termite-chewed survey map we'd found at the Desert View trading post, we made our way across the plateau toward the gorge.

Ceej and Bella led the way, Tim and I trailed a hundred yards behind. When we had to talk to them we would do it at a distance, or I would run ahead to consult with them, then go back to Tim to tell him what was going on. It was frustrating, especially for Tim, but I didn't want him to get any closer.

From the Watchtower, the plateau had looked fairly flat, but once we started walking we quickly learned that flat is a relative term. We were either walking up, down, or around something. We lost the trail several times and had to backtrack. We were not worried about missing the gorge—all we had to do was keep going northeast and we would fall into it. We were trying to follow the Jeep trail because the walking would be easier, and because it would lead us to the Blue Spring Trail, the only way down to the river.

The gorge was only ten miles from the Watchtower, but with all the twists and turns of the Jeep trails we must have walked twice that. After several hours of walking, the trail turned east, and we followed our shadows. As we came up over the top of each low hill we could see the gorge, tantalizingly close but always the same distance away. Then the trail would dip down and we would lose sight of it. The sun was nothing but a faint glow behind us when we spread our blankets beneath the stars, not knowing how close we were to our goal.

Sometime during the night I woke up and found that Tim had rolled up against me in his sleep and thrown one arm over my body. The moon had risen, and I could see the tiny, spiky shadows of eyelashes on his smooth cheeks. I remembered the Tim I had seen facing down Mother K, fierce-eyed and deadly. I could see none of that now. I saw only the gentleness and innocence of a child. I freed one hand from my sleeping bag and laid it as softly as I could upon his cheek. I watched as the man-child, still dreaming, smiled.

I awakened to the scent of distant rain. Moist air cooled my face. I opened my eyes, untangled myself from Tim's embrace, and sat up. The sky glittered with countless stars. I could see no clouds, but a soft, steady breeze came from the north. The rain must have fallen upriver, perhaps as far north as Page.

The moon, low in the west, sank toward the horizon.

I looked at the spot where Ceej and Bella had bedded down. I saw the shape of their blanket, but that was all. I let my eyes explore my surroundings, straining to make sense of the moon-shadowed desert.

There, atop a low rise, something that was not a rock or a shrub. It was the shape of Ceej, standing with his back to me, looking to the north. I stood and walked over to him.

Where is Bella? I asked.

Ceej pointed north. After a moment I saw her. She was about a quarter of a mile away, standing before an uneven, horizontal strip of lighter-colored rock. At first I thought it was a low ridge, but then my mind reinterpreted the image and I realized that she was standing at the edge of a chasm. I was seeing moonlight reflected off the far lip of the gorge.

The Little Colorado.

Ceej nodded. *We were closer than we thought.*

Bella was walking toward us. The breeze had died down. The plateau was nearly silent. I could hear Ceej breathing. He shifted his feet and the sound of his boots on rock seemed startlingly loud. I felt that we were standing on a great ball of rock, a planet, and that we might fly off it at any moment. Bella was growing larger. I took Ceej's hand. He did not pull away. He let me hold his hand as we watched Bella's approach. When she was a few yards away she spoke. Ceej took his hand back.

He moved to embrace her. They exchanged words.

What did she say? I asked.

She has found the trail.

Bella spoke.

Tomorrow we enter the canyon, Ceej translated. *She wants to know if you plan to come with us.*

I am not going to leave you.

She wants to know if you wish to leave this world.

I shook my head. *No thanks.*

Bella nodded, understanding me for once. She spoke.

Ceej interpreted. *She didn't think you would, since you are a Survivor. She says this is your world now. What about Tim?*

Tim is with me, I signed, surprising myself. I could not save Ceej, but there was hope for Tim.

Ceej nodded.

How is she feeling? I asked.

Bella answered my question by coughing once—a

small, delicate clearing of the throat. She may not have been aware that she had done it, but I had heard such coughs before. Over the next two days it would blossom into a juicy, lung-ripping, gurgling hack that would hurt her from the roots of her shorn hair to her cramped toes.

When did she start coughing?

It's just the cold.

We should go back to Desert View. I can take care of her.

No.

If you continue on she will die. And so will you.

If we do not continue on, then we will die.

You can't really believe that, Ceej.

He smiled. *But I do.*

He turned his eyes on me and I saw in that moment how much he had changed. This was not my silly little brother. This Ceej was older and darker and he believed in something bigger than me and Tim and Uncle and Hap and the Grand Canyon. He might be mad as a Kinka, but he had *something.*

Bella touched his arm and spoke.

We should try to sleep, he said to me.

We walked back to our bedrolls. Tim was sitting up, awake.

What's wrong? he asked.

Nothing, I signed. *Go to sleep.*

Faintly, in the distance, I heard Bella cough.

BLUE SPRING

SUN PENETRATED MY EYELIDS. I opened them. Tim's sleeping face was inches away. He looked so young. His eyelids quivered and his lips moved, almost smiling. I wondered what he was dreaming about.

Tim once told me that he remembered nothing of his life before the Flu, even though he had been six years old when the disease struck. He did not remember his mother, or his brother, or his friends. This plague-ridden, corpse-covered world was all he knew. I envied him.

I sat up, trying not to wake him. A transparent mist hung a few feet above the earth, a desert fog that would burn off within the hour. The sky above us was blue, but to the north I saw a dark bank of clouds rising high above the desert. I could still smell rain in the air. I imagined the water falling over the dam at Glen Canyon. It had seemed like such a big deal a few days ago, but now I didn't care. The dam could crumble, the flood could scour the canyon, and I didn't care. Uncle was dead, and my brother would probably be dead soon, and the Glen Canyon Dam seemed like the least of my problems. I looked back at where Ceej and

Bella had bedded down. I could not see them. I stood up and walked closer.

They were gone.

If you took a giant knife blade a mile long, thrust it into the earth, then dragged it, twisting and turning, through a hundred miles of rock, you'd get something like the Little Colorado River Gorge; a rent in the earth as deep as the Grand Canyon, but instead of being ten to twenty miles across, it is only a few hundred yards in some places.

From the brink, looking almost straight down, we could see the weirdly brilliant blue ribbon that was the Little Colorado. It looked impossibly thin and bright, like a thread of blue sky seen through a crack in the earth.

Between us and the river stood a vertical wilderness of rock.

You think they went down there? Tim asked.

I nodded. Somewhere below us, Ceej and Bella were making their way down through that treacherous, rocky maze. Bella's cough would be ripening, and Ceej might be feeling a tickle at the back of his throat.

They are as good as dead, I thought.

I saw Tim staring at me and realized that my hands had spelled out my thought.

Tim signed, *Maybe not.*

You are right, I said. *Maybe not.* Much as I wanted to believe that Ceej and Bella might survive the Flu, I knew that their chances were slim. Mother K had told me that she had brought the Judgment to more than two thousand people and of all those, only three had survived. But there was a chance. I had survived, Mother K had survived—*all* the Kinka were Survivors. As long as there was a chance, I had to be there. Even if Ceej—or Bella—had what it took to survive the Flu, they would need someone to bring them water and feed them and protect them from predators. Even if they were not destined to live they would need someone to make their final hours as comfortable as possible.

If we can find them, I said, *they have a chance.*

For most of the morning we searched for a way down. Several times Tim eased himself over the edge, following a promising-looking ledge, or working his way down a tight crevice, but every time he reached a dead end and had to climb back up. Finally, a half mile upstream, we discovered a rock cairn marking a narrow cut in the lip of the gorge. Looking over the edge, we could see the river and, near the base of the Redwall, a series of blue pools.

That must be Blue Spring, I said.

Tim nodded. *Then this has to be the trail.*

I looked at the steep sides of the crevice. It did not look like a trail to me, but Tim climbed confidently into the cut, feeling his way down with his feet. Within a few seconds he was out of sight and I stood alone at the edge. A few minutes later I heard his voice and saw him waving to me from a ledge fifty feet below the rim. He was telling me to follow him. Trying to remember where Tim had put his feet, I lowered myself over the edge, feeling my way. Several times I thought I was stuck, but then my foot would find a crack in the rock. I worked my way down the crevice one toehold at a time until I reached a wide ledge. The ledge became a steep trail marked with sheep droppings. Moments later I caught up with Tim in the shadow of a bulging limestone wall.

He pointed to a boot print in a patch of loose, sandy dirt.

Ceej, he said.

For the next few hundred yards the trail was clear, following a series of precipitous switchbacks down the limestone wall; then it abruptly disappeared, leaving us to follow a series of cairns along the ragged face of a cliff, using our hands as much as our feet. The river appeared and disappeared as we made our way slowly down. Tim moved easily across the treacherous landscape; his hands and feet seemed to become part of the rock, finding solidity where I saw only instability. I watched where he put his feet, and tried to follow him exactly.

As we descended the steepest part of the gorge, my sense of color warped. The million shades of brown shifted toward red, giving the rocks around us an eerie, pinkish glow; the pools of water below us became an impossibly intense blue. Bluer than the sky, bluer than my mother's eyes.

I caught up with Tim and touched his shoulder. When his eyes were level with mine I asked, *Do the colors look wrong?*

He shook his head, not understanding my signs. I tried again. *Colors different here?*

He nodded vigorously and signed back, speaking as he formed a garbled message with his hands. His signing, literally, came out as *Water color rock hate above green!* But I knew that what he meant was that the colors of the water, the rock, and the plants were all strange-looking. For some reason I always understood what Tim was saying, even when he signed nonsense.

After the first hour or two the route became less steep, and we found ourselves moving along a clearly marked trail. In places the rock gave way to sandy earth, and we could see the prints of my brother's boots, and the smaller marks of Bella's.

At midday we reached Blue Spring, a series of clear pools just above the river. Up close, the water still looked blue, but not as intensely so as it had from the rim. Tim scooped a handful of water and tasted it. He frowned and swallowed. I put my hand in the water. It was cool and it made my skin tingle. I took a cautious sip. The water fizzed on my tongue and had a strong mineral taste. I spat it out. Tim laughed.

I think it's okay, he signed. *It just tastes funny.*

At Blue Spring, the gorge was only a hundred feet across. Millions of years ago the stream had cut a narrow slice through the Redwall layer. I felt as if the earth might close upon us at any moment. Tipping my head back, I looked straight up. The strip of visible sky looked as intensely blue as the river had looked from the rim.

We left the Blue Spring pools behind and, surprisingly quickly, found ourselves standing on a narrow strip of beach with the Little Colorado flowing at our feet. The river banks were crowded with tamarisk, catsclaw acacia, and willows.

Ceej and Bella's footprints, clearly marked in the fine sand, followed the beach downstream, weaving in and out of clumps of grass and groves of stunted trees. Bella's prints showed that her feet were dragging. The stress of the long climb down and the virus raging through her body were bringing her closer to death. In places it looked like Ceej was supporting her. Every time we rounded a bend or climbed a rock outcropping I expected to find them on the other side, Bella slumped in Ceej's arms.

We were about a quarter of a mile downstream from Blue Spring when we lost the trail. Continuing along the beach, we came to a spot where the wall of the gorge bulged in, coming right up to the water, making it impossible to continue on our side.

They must have crossed the river, I said.

The Little Colorado, at that point, was squeezed to

a width of less than twenty feet. Although it was fairly clear, we could not see the bottom, and the water was moving quickly.

Tim indicated that we should backtrack to a place farther upstream. He thought it would be shallower, slower, and easier to cross. A few hundred yards upstream we found Ceej and Bella's footsteps again. We could see where they had entered the water. The stream was almost fifty feet wide there, with a small sandbar poking up in the center.

It looks deep, I said.

Tim nodded, but stepped into the water and began to cross. The water came up to his thighs, but no higher. I followed him to the sandbar, then over to the far side, where we quickly found the trail.

The landscape had become a more muted palette of browns and grays with smudges of dull green. I looked up and saw that the sky had changed color, too—now it was the steely gray of low, moisture-laden clouds.

For the next hour we continued slowly downstream, crossing the river several times. We lost Ceej and Bella's trail twice, but quickly picked it up again.

At one crossing I noticed the sandy river bottom sucking at my boots. Every step took more effort to lift my feet. Tim, a few feet in front of me, was having the same problem. He stopped, and I saw his body go tense with effort. He shouted something, then his left leg came up, then his right, and suddenly he was half-running, half-swimming for the opposite shore. He scrambled up onto the bank. His feet were bare! He turned to me, urgently signing for me to keep moving, to hurry up. I did not have to understand human speech to know the word he was shouting. *Quicksand!*

I tried to increase my pace, but the river bottom wanted me. Lift, step, lift, step. I only had a few yards to go. My feet were sinking ankle-deep, then shin-deep into the quicksand. I saw something waving in front of me. Tim holding out a tree branch. I reached, missed, and fell face first into the river. My hands sank into the sand. I pulled them free and lunged again for the branch, catching it this time, holding tight as Tim slowly pulled me up onto the shore.

We sat on the strip of beach, catching our breath. After a few minutes Tim stood up and looked down at his bare feet.

At least you still have your boots, he said. His had been sucked right off his feet.

Do you think Ceej and Bella got caught in that? I asked.

I hope not.

I touched his bare foot. *Will you be able to walk?*

I don't have any choice, do I?

Something cold struck my shoulder. I looked up. The air above us was fuzzy with rain. Several drops struck my face, and suddenly we were caught in a steady, drenching downpour.

Tim stood up. *Let's keep moving.*

We continued downstream, moving slowly, Tim picking his way gingerly across the sharp rocks. The rain fell upon us ever harder, running down the walls of the gorge and turning the surface of the river into a sheet of furiously dancing droplets. It was late in the day, no more than an hour or two from sunset. The river had lost its turquoise hue and turned to muddy gray. The trail of footprints began to grow faint as the rain beat upon the sand. I wondered what it was like up on the rim. For the rain to fall this hard on the bottom of the gorge, it would have to be a deluge up top.

The Sky in the Hole

CEEJ AND BELLA'S FOOTPRINTS WERE soon lost to us, but we kept walking. It was odd to see Tim, who usually moved so quickly and confidently, picking his way so tentatively over the land. But I was glad to see him being so careful. Here at the bottom of the gorge, a bad cut on his foot could be a death sentence. Our feet were our ticket back to the rim.

We had been following the edge of the river for some time, walking with our heads down to keep the constant rain off our faces, when the ground beneath our feet suddenly changed color.

We had just crossed a small mudflat and were following a rock-studded strip of beach, the water to our left, when we came upon a bright orange and yellow seep. We stopped, puzzled by the unfamiliar colors underfoot. It looked like diluted paint, or some sort of chemical spill. I looked to the right, following the strange, colored water to its source, and there, not ten feet away, rising above us, was a dome of rock thirty feet high.

My first impression was that the dome was a pinkish-gray, but the longer I looked, the more colors

I saw. The water running over the surface of the dome intensified its colors. The rock looked translucent—I thought I could see an underlayer of pale yellow beneath the pinkish-gray surface. The ragged sides of the dome were striped with crusty white deposits, as if a giant had dribbled milk over it. The bottom edge of the dome was undercut where the river had sliced into it during flood stage. Yellow and orange water oozed from the cut beneath the dome and trickled past our feet down to the river.

Tim moved around the base of the dome. I followed, and as I moved the dome's colors became deeper and richer. Red shadows, like spidery veins, appeared at the edge of my vision, but when I looked at them directly they disappeared. The longer I stared at it, the more unreal the dome appeared.

It looked alive.

This was Bella's holy place. It had to be. This was the Sipapuni—but where were Ceej and Bella?

Tim continued around the dome. Afraid to be alone, I hurried to catch up. I found him standing over Ceej's pack, laying on its side in the rain, as if he had simply shrugged it off. My heart felt like a great fist slowly clenching and unclenching in my chest.

Tim shouted something—probably calling Ceej's name. We listened to the sound of rain hissing down. Tim called out again. No one answered. He looked at me, his face streaked with rain.

They have to be here someplace, he signed.

I pointed to the top of the dome, thinking we might see something from up there. Tim dropped his pack and scrambled up the slippery rock. The soles of his bare feet were raw and bleeding. I backed away from the dome, keeping him in sight. At the top he stopped, then squatted down. For several seconds I could not see him at all, then he stood up. I wanted him to look at me and wave, but he stood with his head tipped forward, staring down at something. I was afraid to think what he might be seeing. I opened my mouth and made a sound—I don't know whether it was words or a simple shout. Tim's head jerked up and he turned to face me. He motioned me to join him. I started toward the dome, splashing through ankle-deep water—I had backed right into the river without knowing it. I reached the dome and began to climb. The rock was warm and slippery, but there were plenty of chinks and crevices, and I soon made it to the top.

Tim stood near the apex, at the edge of a shallow basin about eight feet across. I came up beside him. In the center of the depression was a ragged oval aperture about the size of a bathtub. Rain ran into the basin and dripped from the edges of the opening into the interior of the dome.

I think this is it, Tim signed. He got down on his hands and knees and motioned for me to do the same. We crawled to the edge of the hole and looked inside.

Six feet below the rim was a small pool of bluish-gray water, its surface shivered from the droplets falling from the edge of the opening. We could see, faintly, our shadows on the water. Surrounding the pool was a small chamber not quite large enough to stand up in. Tim pointed at something on a ledge at the far side of the pool. At first I did not know what I was looking at, but then I recognized Bella's leather backpack. Next to it was a small cloth sack and, beside that, a pile of yellow powder.

But no Bella; no Ceej.

Tim motioned that he was going down into the chamber.

No! I grabbed his arm.

Tim pulled his arm free. *Ceej and Bella were down there. There has to be some kind of passage, a way out.* He sat down and hung his legs over the edge of the hole.

We don't know that. I had a bad feeling. I did not like this weird rock. I did not want to be separated from Tim, not even by a few yards. *What if something happened to them down there?*

There's only one way to find out. You'll have to help me. He began to lower himself into the hole. His face tightened with effort as he felt with his feet for something solid to stand on. His fingers were white on the slippery rock. He looked at me and shot out a hand, grabbing my wrist. Bracing myself on the rim, I held him, lowering him slowly into the chamber. He found a foothold and some of the weight came off my arm, then he slipped and for a second I was supporting his full weight, but it was too much. His hand slipped down my wrist; he fell with a shout and a splash into the pool.

I thrust my head into the hole and watched him scramble out of the water onto a ledge. The pool was bubbling.

Are you okay?

Tim gave me a thumbs-up.

What do you see? I asked.

He took a moment to look around the chamber. *There's not much here. No other way out.* He crawled around the pool to the backpack. He lifted an object and held it up for me to see. It was a small figurine carved from a piece of wood—I recognized it as a Hopi kachina. Tim returned the kachina to the backpack and turned his attention to the pool. *It looks like some kind of spring. I can see bubbles coming up. There's a funny smell, like electricity.* He scooped up a handful of water and tasted it. *It's fizzy, like at Blue Spring. The air tastes funny.*

I reached down, beckoning.

Just a minute. He moved his face close to the surface of the pool.

I smelled the electric smell now, too. The hairs lifted on the back of my neck.

I see something.

Suddenly the pool began bubbling furiously. Tim stood up. The water in the pool was rising, covering the ledge, climbing up his legs. It looked like he was standing in a huge cauldron of boiling water. Tim looked at me, his face white with terror. The water bubbled around his thighs. I reached in and caught his hand. I lifted, thinking that he was too heavy for me, but fear gave me strength and in an instant he had popped up out of the hole and scrambled onto the top of the dome. We stood up and found ourselves looking at a changed landscape.

The rain was thick and hard. The sky above was dark gray, the gorge had fallen deep into shadow. But the main thing was that the dome, the Sipapuni, was completely surrounded by water. We were standing on a tiny island in the pouring rain, the river flowing around us.

While Tim had been inside the Sipapuni, the river had risen several feet. Instead of a meandering little stream, the Little Colorado had become torrent, red with sediment, filling the gorge with wall to wall water.

Tim and I looked at each other. Water poured from the sky. We could see it climbing the sides of the dome. Within minutes it would come up over the top.

We have to swim for it, Tim said.

Swim to where? This flood will sweep us all the way down to the Grand Canyon.

Tim shook his head and pointed downstream. *That's where it's coming from. It's flowing backwards.*

I shook my head, confused.

It's not the rain, he said. *It's the dam. The dam broke. Look.* He pointed at the water. *It's red. This is Colorado River water.*

He was right, but there was no time to think about what that meant. The river water was only a few feet below us; the rain was coming down so hard we could hardly see the walls of the gorge. I looked down at the hole at our feet and saw a boiling cauldron of blue and orange and yellow, rising. Then, for a single frozen instant, the surface of the water crystallized and I was looking down through a shimmering window. Far below, between thick lumps of cloud, I saw a turquoise ribbon of river, its shores crowded with mesquite and acacia, winding through a deep canyon. We were moving down through the clouds, falling. I gasped and grabbed Tim, unable to tear my eyes from the hole as the ghost river rushed toward us with dizzying speed. The surface of the pool exploded, sending a bubbling riot of colors up through the hole, pouring over our feet, running down the sides of the dome. Tim shouted something, pulling me away from the aperture. Suddenly we were in the river, swept away in a whirl of rain, rock, and river. I paddled frantically, trying to keep my head above water. I saw Tim's head a few yards away and swam toward him, but then lost sight of him as an eddy caught me and spun me around. I couldn't tell whether I was headed upstream or downstream or toward the walls, but I kept swimming, tossed about by sudden changes in the current as the water moved the wrong way through the gorge. I imagined myself dashed against the sharp rocks of the canyon walls, sucked into a whirlpool, knocked on the head by a hunk of debris, or simply swimming with no place to land until I became too exhausted to keep my head above water and sank slowly to rest on the river bottom. My arms were hurting and my breath came in gasps. I was sure I was about to die when I heard a sound like a human voice. Was it Tim, or thunder echoing through the gorge? It came again. I changed direction and headed for the sound, kicking and paddling with new energy. The water swirling around me and splashing in my face and the rain pouring down made it impossible to see. Was I moving forward or being swept away? Again, I heard Tim calling out to me. My arms were like logs, my legs floppy as rubber bands, but I kept swimming, moving toward the sound of his voice.

THE WORLD

I REMEMBER TIM'S HAND ON my wrist, pulling me out of the water. I remember climbing, clawing our way up the sides of the gorge, struggling to stay above the rising flood waters, Tim's voice urging me onward. At some point the river peaked and we found ourselves wedged into a deep crevice. The last shreds of daylight disappeared. We spent the night clinging to each other for warmth, too exhausted and terrified to sleep.

By first light the flood had subsided. Dawn came bright and clear and cool. We were near the top of the Redwall, a few hundred feet above the canyon floor. The walls of the gorge and the banks of the river were covered with mud and debris. Mesquite and tamarisk trees drooped, stripped of their leaves and coated with fine red silt. The river, opaque with sediment, snaked through the muddy wreckage.

The Sipapuni had disappeared, leaving behind only bare, muddy beach.

Tim and I began to climb, inching our way slowly up the crevice. It seemed impossible, but since we had no choice, we climbed. By the time the sun appeared over the rim, we had found a sheep trail. Tim's feet were a mass of cuts and scrapes. I tore the sleeves from my shirt and wrapped them.

By midday we had reached the rim. Looking down at the flood-ravaged gorge, it was almost impossible to believe that Ceej and Bella were still alive. But then, we should not have survived either.

What do you think happened to them? Tim asked.

I didn't answer him right away. I had seen something in the Sipapuni. Another canyon; another river. Had it been real, or a hallucination?

What did you see in the pool? I asked.

I thought I saw a bird, Tim signed.

Is that all?

Clouds.

I nodded. *Maybe Bella was right. Maybe they passed through.*

Through to what?

I swept my arms through the air to include the gorge, the plateau, the sky. *Maybe to this.*

Tim stared at me.

Maybe we passed through, too, I said. *Doesn't the world feel different to you?*

Tim shook his head. *No!*

Then what happened to the Sipapuni?

The flood washed it away.

A rock bigger than a house? I don't think so. I pointed down. *That was where Blue Springs was. Now there is nothing but mud-covered rock.*

Tim stared into the gorge.

It even smells different, I said.

The air was crisp and clean and fresh with the smell of wet grasses and trees, the blue of the sky was almost painful in its purity, and the sun seemed larger and more golden than before. A faint haze rose from the rain-soaked desert.

Tim was shaking his head. He would not leave his world behind so easily.

I don't believe it, he said.

I wasn't sure I believed it either. Maybe the river *had* washed away the Sipapuni. Maybe Blue Springs was simply concealed beneath a layer of mud. Maybe the sun was the same sun and the air smelled different only because of the rain. Maybe Ceej and Bella were dead on the river bottom, their mouths filled with silt.

Wherever we were, we both knew that we had to move on. We would not survive another night without food and shelter. I retied the makeshift bandages on Tim's feet. Hungry and tired, the sun warming our backs, we headed east, following the rim of the gorge. In another twenty miles we would come to the ruins of a town called Cameron where amid the long-dead corpses and ghosts we would find clothing and shelter and ancient cans of food.

If Cameron was there.

If not, one way or another, we would survive.

Author's Notes

The Sipapuni

The Sipapuni is real. It is a large travertine limestone dome located in the Little Colorado Gorge approximately five miles above the point where the Little Colorado River flows into the Grand Canyon. The dome was formed by a mineral-rich spring many tens of thousands of years ago.

Many Hopis believe that their ancestors emerged from an aperture at the top of the Sipapuni, a gateway from the Third World to this, the Fourth World.

It is one of their most sacred places.

The Flu

Everybody has been sick with influenza. Usually it makes a person miserable for a week or so, then goes away. But not all strains of the flu are the same. In 1918, an influenza epidemic killed one hundred million people, many of them young, healthy adults. No one knows for sure what made the 1918 flu so deadly, but most experts agree on one thing: It could happen again.